Peter Cheyney and The Murder Room

>>> This title is part of The Murder Room, our series dedicated to making available out-of-print or hard-to-find titles by classic crime writers.

Crime fiction has always held up a mirror to society. The Victorians were fascinated by sensational murder and the emerging science of detection; now we are obsessed with the forensic detail of violent death. And no other genre has so captivated and enthralled readers.

Vast troves of classic crime writing have for a long time been unavailable to all but the most dedicated frequenters of second-hand bookshops. The advent of digital publishing means that we are now able to bring you the backlists of a huge range of titles by classic and contemporary crime writers, some of which have been out of print for decades.

From the genteel amateur private eyes of the Golden Age and the femmes fatales of pulp fiction, to the morally ambiguous hard-boiled detectives of mid twentieth-century America and their descendants who walk our twenty-first century streets, The Murder Room has it all. **>>>**

The Murder Room
Where Criminal Minds Meet

themurderroom.com

Peter Cheyney (1896–1951)

Reginald Evelyn Peter Southouse Cheyney was born in Whitechapel in the East End of London. After serving as a lieutenant during the First World War, he worked as a police reporter and freelance investigator until he found success with his first Lemmy Caution novel. In his lifetime Cheyney was a prolific and wildly successful author, selling, in 1946 alone, over 1.5 million copies of his books. His work was also enormously popular in France, and inspired Jean-Luc Godard's character of the same name in his dystopian sci-fi film *Alphaville*. The master of British noir, in Lemmy Caution Peter Cheyney created the blueprint for the tough-talking, hard-drinking pulp fiction detective.

By Peter Cheyney

Lemmy Caution Novels
This Man Is Dangerous (1937)
Poison Ivy (1937)
Dames Don't Care (1937)
Can Ladies Kill? (1938)
Don't Get Me Wrong (1939)
You'd Be Surprised (1940)
Your Deal, My Lovely (1941)
Never a Dull Moment (1942)
You Can Always Duck (1942)
I'll Say She Does (1946)

Slim Callaghan Novels
The Urgent Hangman (1938)
Dangerous Curves (1939)
You Can't Keep the Change
 (1940)
It Couldn't Matter Less (1941)
Sorry You've Been Troubled
 (1942)
They Never Say When (1944)

Uneasy Terms (1946)
Dance Without Music (1947)
Calling Mr Callaghan (1953)

The 'Dark' Series
Dark Duet (1942)
 aka *The Counterspy Murders*
The Stars Are Dark (1943)
 aka *The London Spy Murders*
The Dark Street (1944)
 aka *The Dark Street Murders*
Sinister Errand (1945)
 aka *Sinister Murder*
Dark Hero (1946)
 aka *The Case of the Dark Hero*
Dark Interlude (1947)
 aka *The Terrible Night*
Dark Wanton (1948)
 aka *Case of the Dark Wanton*
Dark Bahama (1950)
 aka *I'll Bring Her Back*

Sinister Errand

Peter Cheyney

Copyright © 1945 Peter Cheyney

The right of Peter Cheyney to be identified as the author of the work has been asserted in accordance with the Copyright, Designs and Patents Act 1988.

This edition published in
The Crime Bibliophile from THE MURDER ROOM

Originally...
...in Great Britain by...

London WC2H 9EA

An Hachette UK company.

All rights reserved. No part of this publication...

ISBN 978 1 4719 0179 9

This is a work of fiction. Names, characters, places, organisations and incidents are either the product of the author's imagination or used fictitiously.

No part of this publication may be reproduced, stored in a retrieval system, or transmitted in any form or by any means without the prior written permission of the publisher, nor be otherwise circulated in any form of binding or cover other than that in which it is published and without a similar condition being imposed on the subsequent purchaser.

www.themurderroom.com

An Orion book

Copyright © Peter Cheyney 1945

The right of Peter Cheyney to be identified as the author of this work has been asserted in accordance with the Copyright, Designs and Patents Act 1988.

This edition published by
The Orion Publishing Group Ltd
Orion House
5 Upper St Martin's Lane
London WC2H 9EA

An Hachette UK company
A CIP catalogue record for this book is available from the British Library

ISBN 978 1 4719 0179 9

www.orionbooks.co.uk

CONTENTS

CONTENTS

MEMORY UNLIMITED

I JUMPED into the first railway compartment which seemed empty, without noticing the little companion that was pre-destined to keep me awake all night. The train moved slowly out of the station. I gazed at the lights of Stockholm gently receding into the darkness, wrapped my rug around me and prepared to go to sleep. My eyes fell on a book left on the seat opposite by a previous passenger.

I took it up absent-mindedly and ran through the first few lines. Five minutes later, I was reading it as eagerly as a clue to a hidden treasure.

I learned that everyone's memory is capable of fantastic feats, that the least gifted of people can memorise once and for all, information as complicated as a list of the hundred largest towns in the world and their populations, all this after reading it through once only.

It seemed unlikely then that I should succeed in filing away the interminable lists of figures, dates, towns, their populations and reigning families, which had driven me to despair during my school days, when my memory was fresh. I thought I would test the truth of the statement.

I took a time-table out of my suitcase and began reading quietly in the manner prescribed, the names of the hundred railway stations between Stockholm and Trehorningsjo.

I observed that after reading it over only once, I really could recite that list in the order I had read it, and in its reverse order. I could even point out immediately the relative position of any town, for instance, which was the 27th, the 84th and the 36th, so deeply were these names imprinted in my mind.

I was astonished at the memory I had acquired and spent the rest of the night making new and more difficult experiments without reaching the limits of what I was so quickly capable.

I did not, of course, confine myself to experiments and on the next day I put to practical use my knowledge of the laws of the mind. I was then able to memorise with surprising ease whatever I read, the music I heard, the names and faces of people who called on me, their addresses, my business appointments, and even to learn Spanish in four months.

If I have obtained from life a measure of wealth and happiness, it is to that book I owe it, for it revealed to me the workings of my brain.

Three years ago, I had the good fortune to meet its author and I promised him to propagate his method, and today I am glad of this opportunity of expressing my gratitude to him.

I can only suppose that others wish to acquire, what is, after all, the most valuable asset towards success in life. Borg's address is L. A. Borg, c/o Aubanel Publishers, 14 Lower Baggott Street, Dublin.

Apply to him for his little book, *The Eternal Laws of Success*. It is free to all who wish to develop their memory.   F. ROBERTS.

CHAPTER ONE

THE HEAP OF FEATHERS

KALEIDOSCOPIC pictures of last night's party presented themselves between myself and the ceiling. One or two faces—one of them was certainly Sammy's face, the other that of an attractive woman—flashed across my memory. I felt a little sick and did not want particularly to think about them. In fact I did not want to think about anything.

You wouldn't get any funny ideas about me, would you? You wouldn't come to the conclusion that I was just another of those people who've become bored with the war and try to " sublimate " their annoyance by getting cockeyed all the time? I'm not a bit like that. But —and I think I should point this out *now*—when one has been in the sort of racket that I've been playing around in for the last few years, it's a very good thing for a man to relax occasionally—*if* you get me—just to stop himself going entirely nuts.

I lay looking at the ceiling. The back of my neck felt as if I had been wearing an iron clamp. There were spots in front of my eyes and my tongue felt as if somebody had gone over it with a piece of sandpaper. I felt like nothing on earth. I lay there making up my mind that I'd get up somehow.

Eventually I did. I sat on the edge of the bed looking at the disordered bedroom. My clothes were strewn all over the place. My black soft hat was perched precariously on the head of a small bust of Napoleon that stood on the mantelpiece. There was only one thing to do about it. I got to my feet ; found my trousers and felt in the hip pocket. It's a funny thing but no matter how cockeyed I am, I usually manage to collect a pint of whisky. Sure enough the flask was there—and full ! I unscrewed it and took a long stiff drink. It made me shudder but it pulled me together.

I went back ; sat on the bed ; considered the situation.

I tried to sort out details of the party. I wasn't very successful. I'd arrived expecting something important to happen ; that Sammy was really going to start something. Instead of which I found him so cockeyed that it was just nobody's business. Why? After which I proceeded to do a little drinking myself.

Then there was that girl. I had a vague idea about her. I remember her as a personality, but I couldn't remember what she looked like. I'd talked to her. Was she with Sammy or wasn't she? I didn't know.

And I had an odd idea about Sammy. Sammy didn't seem to *want* to talk to me. Most peculiar that. Somewhere at the back of my aching head was an impression that I'd tried once or twice to get something out of him. I also had the idea that he'd been very disinclined for anything of the sort.

All very odd and peculiar.

My watch was on the dressing-table. I walked over and looked at it. It was six o'clock—a lovely summer's evening. Somewhere I could hear a " doodle-bug " flying. I suppose I'd been asleep when the alert went.

I began to think about the Old Man. What the hell was he playing at ? Directly I'd got off the boat yesterday I'd telephoned him. All I could get from him was that I was to see Sammy as soon as I could and then take it easy ; and keep away from the Old Man. It seemed as if he was being damned leery about something. I wondered what.

I began to feel a little better. I went into the bathroom ; took a hot shower and then a cold one. Then I rang downstairs for some coffee—strong black coffee. I shaved, unpacked some fresh clothes and dressed myself. I dressed rather carefully because I felt that after last night I'd better do something to get my morale cracking. Everybody drinks a lot in wartime, but it seemed to me that I must have drunk enough to float a couple of battleships. I still felt a little dizzy.

I was nearly dressed when the coffee came up. I drank it, began to pick up my clothes. More out of habit than anything else I went through the pockets. Sometimes after I've been to parties I've found something there before—a visiting card or something—you never know.

2

In my left lower waistcoat pocket was a piece of paper and written on it was : " S—23 *Kinnoul Street, S.W.*1."

I grinned. That was a little better. It seemed that I'd had enough sense to skewer Sammy's address out of him. I began to think about Sammy. It seemed the best thing I could do would be to go round there right away, have a meal with him and talk.

I took my hat off Napoleon—a process which made him look a great deal more serious—and went out. As I got out into the street the " All Clear " went. It was a nice fresh evening. As I walked along I began to feel better. My circulation speeded up a little and my head cleared.

I walked to Kinnoul Street. The street was an old-fashioned street with rather nice houses that looked like good class apartment houses on each side. No. 23 had been freshly painted. I rang the bell and when nothing happened knocked on the door. I stood there for about five minutes ; then I gave the door a push. It was open, so I went in. I closed the door behind me and stood in the hallway and coughed and made the usual noises. Then I called : " Is anyone there ? " But nothing happened.

I went to the top of the basement stairs, opened the door and called some more. The place was quite silent. I went back into the hallway, I looked into a sitting-room on the right of the front door. Then I began to walk up the carpeted staircase. There was a landing halfway up with a room on each side. I opened a door and looked in. It was Sammy's bedroom all right. I recognised the tie hanging over the mirror on the dressing-table. When I saw it I remembered it from last night. I'd admired it. It was a nice heavy Spitalfields silk tie in grey and black —the sort of dressy thing Sammy goes in for.

The room looked worse than mine had looked when I woke. It looked as if somebody had driven a Bren-gun-carrier over it. There were clothes and shoes all over the place. There was a half bottle of brandy, a glass and a half-used siphon on the dressing-table. Obviously Sammy had been doing a little additional drinking.

I began to think about Sammy. I walked round the room, stepping over odd articles of clothing. Then I went back to the dressing-table and I saw something that seemed a little odd to me.

In the centre of the table was a black ebony bowl—the sort of thing you use to put studs in. But there weren't any studs in it. In the middle was a little pile of white swansdown. I wondered about that. I went over to the bed, which had been slept in, and I could see that somebody had slit one end of one of the pillows. A little more swandsown was sticking out of the hole.

I lit a cigarette. I was drawing my first lungful of smoke when the door opened and a woman came in. A nice looking woman of somewhere about forty years of age with a clear complexion and very blue eyes. She had a hat on and had obviously just come in.

She said : " Well, you've made yourself at home pretty quickly. Can I do something for you ? " Her voice was well-bred and she clipped her words concisely.

I said : " Thanks. You can. I came here to see my friend."

She said : " You mean Mr. Carew ? "

I said : " That's right. I mean Mr. Carew. I rang the bell and did all the normal things, found the door open, came in and yelled. Nothing happened, so I investigated. Do you know where he is ? I want him rather urgently."

She said in a flat sort of voice : " How urgently ? " She didn't sound as if she were trying to be funny or anything.

I said : " Well, his aunt was killed this afternoon by one of those ' doodle-bugs.' " It was the first thing I could think of.

She said : " Well, I didn't know he had another aunt, but I suppose if you say so . . ."

I said : " What do you mean—another aunt ? "

She said : " Well, I happen to be Sammy's aunt, you see. That's all."

I grinned at her. I said : " Well, that's very funny, isn't it ? The other one—the one he told me about—must have been not his aunt. Perhaps she was his cousin. Anyway, do you know where he is ? "

She said : " No, I don't. All I know is that he came in at an early hour this morning so drunk that I thought he'd

4

pass out at any moment. I came up the stairs just now expecting to find him still asleep. Quite obviously, he's got up and gone out. But I don't know where he's gone to."

"Therefore," I said, " you won't know when he'll be back ? "

She nodded.

I said : " Look, is there a pub or a place somewhere round here called The Feathers ? "

She said : " Yes, there is. That's an idea. He might have gone there to have a ' hair of the dog that bit him.' There's a place round in Mulbery Street—just round the corner. It's called The Heap of Feathers."

I said : " Thank you very much. If I find him I'll bring him back in good order."

She stood aside as I moved over to the doorway. When I got there I said to her : " I think Sammy's pretty lucky to have an aunt like you. I think you've *got* something."

She said : " I'll tell you one thing, young man. You've got a hell of a nerve, haven't you ? "

" I'm not so young," I said, " but I hope my nerve's all right. Bye-bye, Auntie ! "

I went down the stairs and out into the street. Actually I didn't like it at all. Not one little bit.

Mulbery Street was " one of those " places. A place with an atmosphere that, for some inexplicable reason, did something to you. I expect you know what I mean. That kind of street that strikes a memory chord in your mind although you've never seen or heard of it before.

Here it was, right in the middle of London, with the Piccadilly traffic not five minutes away. Yet it was quiet and the street might have been set in the heart of the country. It was an odd crooked street with little houses. One of them was painted blue. There were four public houses in the street—old-fashioned little places with signs hanging outside. The second sign down the street had the words " The Heap of Feathers " painted on it. I could read it quite easily.

I wasn't feeling particularly happy. I was a little worried about the way things were going. The great thing was I wanted to have a talk with Sammy—to get things straightened up with him.

There were four or five stone steps leading into the saloon bar of the Heap of Feathers, which was in a little passage just off the street. The bar was very small. There were half a dozen people in it. Standing in the corner, working out a crossword puzzle, was a young man with black hair and a thin white face. I had the impression that he was wearing some make-up. His clothes were fancy and much too well-cut. A pansy, I thought !

There was a man with one arm who was drinking a pint of bitter beer out of a glass mug in sips ; there was a blonde woman—a rather nice looking woman—whose skirt was too tight and too short who was sitting on a high stool showing more than the standard allowance of leg. She was quite cockeyed and seemed very happy about it. In the corner opposite to the pansy was a young man in a rough tweed coat with a Merchant Navy badge in the lapel. There were two other nondescript men talking about racing in a corner. But no Sammy.

After a minute, a pleasant faced woman came into the bar. I ordered a glass of beer. When she brought it I said : " Perhaps you can help me. I expected to meet a friend round here—name of Carew. He's tall, very good looking, fair haired, rather thin, attractive, face. I wonder if you've seen him. I thought perhaps he might have left a message for me."

She shook her head. She said : " I believe I've seen your friend some time. I seem to remember him by your description. But I haven't seen him this evening."

I said : " Thank you." I felt a peculiarly heavy sense of disappointment. I finished my beer and turned towards the door. I was nearly through when the pansy said in a rather high falsetto voice :

" Oh, excuse me, but I might be able to help you. Your friend was in here about an hour ago."

The woman behind the bar said : " Yes, he might have been here then. I was upstairs. I wouldn't have seen him." She said to the white-faced young man : " Did he leave any message ? '

He said : " I don't think so. He went off with Janine."

6

I moved over towards my effeminate young friend. I gave him a charming smile. I said : " You're being very helpful. I suppose you wouldn't know where he and Janine were going ? "

He smiled cynically. He said : " Well, I could make a guess. I should think they were going to Janine's place."

I said : " I see. And would you know where Janine's place is ? "

He smiled. It wasn't a particularly nice smile. He said : " I should think everybody knows that. Anyway, if you go straight up to the end of Mulbery Street and turn to the right you come to a place called Daisy Place. Go across it, and there's a little street on the other side— Verity Street." He simpered a little. " It's quite a nice street—most amusing—old houses and all that. Janine lives at No. 16, I think."

I said : " Thank you very much. Would you care for a drink ? "

He said : " That's very kind of you. The only thing is I'm inclined to be expensive. I like brandy and soda."

I said : " Have a brandy and soda by all means. I'll have one myself."

I ordered two brandies and sodas. When he put his hand up on the bar to take the glass I noticed he was wearing a signet ring on the little finger of his left hand, but the ring was turned inwards so that one could only see the gold band. It was a flat band. There was a mark on it as if someone had tried to file it.

He said : " Well, cheerio ! Thank you for the drink."

We drank the brandy. I said good-night and I went out.

The sun seemed to have disappeared. The atmosphere was rather depressing and grey. Walking along I wondered what the hell was the matter anyway. I seemed to be behaving like an old lady with the jitters.

I began to think about Sammy. A peculiar one that one. You were never *absolutely* certain where you were with Sammy. I don't mean that he was weak or fatuous or anything like that, but he had a way of flying off at a tangent. He used to say that there was method in his madness. Maybe there was, but in this particular case I thought he was rather giving me the run-around—and for what? He knew damned well what the Old Man had said, yet here he was playing around with this Janine piece—whoever she might be—amusing himself, while I didn't even know which way I was pointing. Or was he amusing himself?

I arrived at 16 Verity Street. It was a narrow street, old-fashioned and clean, and the houses were a good sixty or seventy years old. No. 16 had some flower boxes on the ground-floor window-sill. I went up the three stone steps and stood looking at the bell-pushes on the right hand side of the door. There were three—Ground, First and Second floors—and underneath each one in metal frame affixed to the wall was a visiting card. The middle card said: "'Janine' 16 Verity Street." Just that—nothing else.

I punched the bell and waited. After a minute there was a click and the front door opened a bit. It had been opened from the first floor by one of those remote control switch things. I pushed open the door and went up the stairs. The stairs curved round to the right and on the first floor landing, leaning against the door-post of one of the two rooms was a woman.

What a piece! A hell of a piece, I'm telling *you*. Although she looked as if she didn't give a damn whether you thought so or not. I've never seen a woman look so bored in my life. But she'd got plenty of everything it takes and she was worth taking a long look at. Definitely a personality.

She was an ash-blonde—real, not a peroxide one—and she had violet eyes. Her hair was naturally waved and a little untidy. But it hung attractively over her shoulder tied with a ribbon. She was wearing a sapphire-blue shantung silk housecoat that came down to the floor, with rose-coloured collar, cuffs and sash. The way she was leaning against the door-post caught the thin silk close against her thigh and outlined a shape that was *very* good. She had on rose-coloured velvet mules with very high heels and very sheer suntan silk stockings. Where the housecoat had opened a little I could see a *vieux rose* suspender.

I thought: Well . . . well . . . well . . . Sammy certainly does find 'em. He certainly does.

I said good-evening. I told her I was looking for a friend called Sammy Carew. I said I'd been told he was here.

She looked at me for a bit without saying anything. Her eyes were sombre. She looked as if something was getting her rather badly.

She said : " Was Sammy Carew a friend of yours ? "

I nodded. " How do you mean—*was* ? " I asked.

She pushed herself away from the doorpost. She pushed herself away from it with her shoulder and, as she turned one beautifully moulded leg came out of the housecoat. I've seen some very good legs in my time but this one had the best pair I've ever come across. Altogether she was a hell of a dish. I was beginning to get a little interested in her myself.

She said : " You'd better come in." She had a husky voice—a low and very soft sort of voice—and she spoke in a rather lazy manner that indicated that she didn't give a damn whether she said anything or whether you listened if she did.

She went into the room. I crossed the landing and went in after her. I stood in the doorway, with my soft hat in my hand, looking at her and the room.

The room was pretty good. It was large, very clean and well-dusted, and very nicely furnished. It was the sitting-room of a person of taste. The walls were primrose ; there were one or two good prints and quite a lot of flowers. I wondered where she could get that quantity of flowers in July 1944, but after a second's consideration I came to the conclusion that some man was probably cashing in with them. After all, if a man is stuck on a woman he gets flowers *somehow*. And she was the sort of woman that ninety-nine men out of a hundred would be well and truly stuck on. The hundredth man would have to be blind or stupid.

She stood in the middle of the room looking at me. She was relaxed and poised but she looked faintly worried and fearfully bored with everything—including me.

She said : " If Sammy Carew was a good friend of yours this isn't going to sound so good to you." She looked as if she was about to yawn, and put her long fingers over her mouth. She was wearing a couple of diamond rings

9

that had cost quite a lot of money. However, she decided not to yawn. Instead : " You'd better sit down, hadn't you ? " she said. " If you want a cigarette, there's one in the box on the little table."

I said thank you and sat down by the little table. I took one of the cigarettes and lit it. It was a good Turkish cigarette—fat and expensive.

I waited. She stood quietly in the middle of the room, looking at me. She said : " You aren't *very* interested or curious, are you ? You don't seem at all excited to know about Sammy Carew. Or don't you care ? "

I shrugged my shoulders. I said : " I don't see what that's got to do with you, Janine. I'm just waiting to hear all about it. I'm a very patient type."

She said casually : " I didn't tell you you could call me Janine. . . ."

I said : " I don't mind what I call you. But you've got Janine on the card by the door downstairs and if you don't want to be called that you ought to have your proper name on the card."

She didn't reply to that one. She moved, gracefully, to the settee on the other side of the room and sat down. When she sat down some more leg appeared. I realised that this wasn't done deliberately. She just didn't care if she showed some leg. I began to think that this Janine was wasting her time at 16 Verity Street. She could have made a million in pictures.

She got up, came over to the table, helped herself to a cigarette, lit it with a lighter produced from her housecoat pocket, went back to the settee and sat down again. This time she *saw* that she was showing some leg so she casually covered it with the housecoat.

She said : " Carew came here very early this morning —about four o'clock. I'm not certain of the time. He was here about an hour. Then he went off. Apparently when he left the house a War Reserve policeman saw him go. He went up the street, turned into Fells Street and then started to cross the Square. The policeman, who was at the top of the street by this time, could see him crossing the Square. Just as he was passing the place where some road repairs are being done, a flying bomb came over and dropped in the Square. The truck belonging to the road repair people was blown over and Carew was underneath. When the policeman got there he was dead. So the policeman came back here and told me about it. He thought I was a relative—or something like that."

I said : "So he was killed by the truck being blown on top of him ? "

She shrugged her shoulders. "Who knows ? " she asked. "The policeman said that he must have been dead before the truck hit him—the blast *must* have killed him."

I got up. I said : "Thanks a lot. I suppose he's in the local mortuary ? "

She shrugged her shoulders. "I suppose so," she said.

I picked up my hat. I said : "I'm grateful to you for being so helpful. I suppose Sammy was a great friend of yours ? "

She got up. She stood looking at me with half-closed eyes. She said : "Do you ? "

I moved over to the door. "Thanks for the cigarette, Janine," I said. "I hope we meet again."

She was standing in the middle of the floor. The cigarette, held between the fingers of the left hand, that hung by her side, sent up a spiral of smoke.

She said slowly : "Well . . . if you want to I suppose you will."

I smiled at her. "You really think that ? " I asked.

"Most people do what they want in the long run," she said. "People like you, I mean. . . ."

I asked : "What do you mean by people like me ? "

She made a movement with her hand. The smoke spiral from the cigarette was broken. She said : "Must we become involved in long discussions about things. I'm very tired. Good-bye."

I smiled at her again. I said good-bye and went down the stairs. I closed the front door carefully behind me and began to walk towards Fells Street.

I'd been right in my idea that things weren't so good.

When I got outside I looked at my watch. It was eight-thirty. I walked down Verity Street and into the

Square I could see the place where the flying bomb had fallen. It was railed off and a repair section was at work. I walked over and asked one of the men where the nearest police station was. He told me and I went along there.

The station sergeant was agreeable and sympathetic. I said : "A relative of mine—a cousin named Carew—was killed early this morning by one of these flying bombs —the one that came down in the Square. I thought I ought to make a proper identification."

He said he'd look into it and went away. I leaned up against the desk and smoked a cigarette.

When he came back he said : "That's quite right. Apparently somebody—a civilian—saw him come out of a house in Verity Street. He saw him go across the Square just about the time the 'doodle-bug' came down. It blew a truck that was in the square on top of him. He could have been killed either by the bomb or the truck. If you'd like to see him he's round in the mortuary. I'll take you round there. By the way, could I have your name and address ? "

I produced an identity card ; then we went round to the mortuary.

It was Sammy all right. His face was practically untouched. He looked better looking than ever, I thought. The rest of him was covered over with a blanket. I stood there looking at him, thinking about the old days. I thought it was a bit tough that Sammy who'd been in so many tight corners should be finished by Mr. Hitler's V1. I wondered exactly what he'd had on him when he died ; whether there was anything he wouldn't have liked found.

I said to the Sergeant : "I suppose there were some effects ? "

He said : "Yes." He looked at Sammy. "You're satisfied about him ? "

I said : "Yes, that's Carew. There's no question about it."

He asked : "Are you the next of kin or is there anybody else ? "

I said : "Yes, there's an aunt. I didn't want to worry

her about it till I was quite certain. I'll let her know about it."

He said : " By the way, I'd like you to look at some of the things we found on him. Strangely enough, he had two identity cards, both of which seemed to be legitimate. One is in the name of Carew, and the other in another name. I suppose you wouldn't know anything about that ? "

I said : " No, I wouldn't know anything about that."

He went to a drawer and produced a silk handkerchief ; I remembered it—a rather nice Chinese silk thing that Sammy had had a long time. He brought it over and put it on the desk. There was a rather badly torn pocketbook, a few coins, a twisted tiepin and a .38 Colt Automatic. I looked at the things.

The Sergeant said : " I wonder what he was carrying a gun for."

I said I wouldn't know. I said that Carew had been a rather dramatic sort of person—one of those people who like carrying pistols. I picked the gun up and took the clip out. I looked at it : slipped it back again.

I said : " I wonder why it is men want to carry automatic pistols. I suppose it's a theatrical habit."

He nodded. He wrapped the things up in the silk handkerchief ; put them back in the drawer.

I said : " You've been very kind. I'll go off now and have a word with his aunt. I expect she'll come round. You'll want all the ends properly tied up."

He said it would be rather nice if she could.

I said good-evening, went out of the police station, walked down the road until I found a bar. I went in and bought myself a large whisky and soda. I drank it slowly and wondered what I was going to do about Sammy and one or two other things. The situation looked as if it was going to be very difficult, I thought. If I got in touch with the Old Man he'd probably be damned annoyed. He gets like that. He expects people to work out their own salvation and I couldn't see myself working out anything at all on this job.

I had another whisky and soda, walked around for a bit until I found a telephone call box, went inside and rang the Old Man. His voice came over the wire as terse and acid as ever.

I said : " Listen, I'm not very happy about anything. I want to talk to you."

He said : " For God's sake—what do you have to talk to me for ? I thought you were intelligent. You've got the reputation for being intelligent anyway. What's the matter ? Haven't you seen Carew ? "

I said : " No, and I'm afraid I shan't have the opportunity either."

There was a pause ; then he said : " I see. All right. I'll be at the Half Moon, off Bruton Street, in fifteen minutes' time. There's a little private bar at the back."

I said : " All right," and hung up.

It took me the fifteen minutes to walk to Bruton Street. I went into the Half Moon, through the saloon bar into the private bar on the other side. I bought myself a drink and carried it over to the table in the corner where the Old Man was sitting. He'd got a large glass of port in front of him. His face was more lined than ever, but his hands were still young looking and strong. Standing there, looking at him, I thought he was a rather marvellous old boy when you came to consider it ; he hadn't aged much since I'd seen him last, two years before.

He said : " Sit down. What's all this damned nonsense about Carew ? "

I said : " It's not a bit of good losing your temper. It's not going to get anybody anywhere. Here's the story. After I spoke to you on the telephone I called Sammy. I got through to him because he hadn't telephoned me. He was going to a party. He told me to meet him there. This was last night. Well, I went there. It was quite a good party—the usual sort of thing—you know, some very attractive women and a lot of liquor . . ."

He interrupted. He said : " You didn't get a chance to talk to him ? "

" That's right," I said. " I think he'd had a couple. I tried to get him into a corner once or twice, but he didn't want to talk."

The Old Man said : " Probably he didn't want to talk there. Maybe he was scared of something."

I raised my eyebrows. " I wonder what would scare Sammy," I said.

The Old Man looked at me. His eyes were a little tired, I thought.

He said : " He was scared all right about something. All right, what happened then ? "

I said: " Well, when I saw that we weren't going to get down to any sort of business I suppose I got drunk too. I went home. I got up late this afternoon. I'd got his address written down on a piece of paper in my pocket. I went round there. It looked as if he'd got up in a hurry. I looked around to see if he'd left any sort of tip-off and I found a little pile of swansdown in a tray on the dressing-table. There was a woman round there—a nice looking woman. She suggested he might be at a pub called The Heap of Feathers. I went round there. There I got on to another place he'd been to. He'd been there with a woman, Apparently he left there early this morning. Some civilian saw him leave the place ; saw him turn across into the Square. Then a flying bomb came down and a repair truck was blown on top of him. That was the end of him."

The Old Man never batted an eyelid. He said : " Have you seen him ? "

I nodded. " I've just left the mortuary," I said. " It was Sammy all right."

The Old Man sighed. He said : " It's not so good, is it ? "

I looked at him. " Isn't it ? " I said. " Why isn't it ? "

He said : " The trouble is I don't know what Sammy was doing. He was sent down here by you know who. He got in touch with me the day before yesterday. He told me he was on to something pretty big. He asked if you were around. I said we were expecting you back off the boat some time soon. He said if you arrived for you to be put in touch with him. He'd talk to you about it and you could let me know. He said there wasn't any time to be lost. He'd got to get a ripple on. He didn't particularly want to contact me. Now you know as much as I do."

I said : " Well, it sounds like one of those nice intelligent obvious set-ups . . . I don't think. Nobody knows anything about anything except Sammy—and he's dead."

The Old Man finished his glass of port. He picked it up, took my empty glass, went to the bar, ordered more drinks, brought them back. He put my whisky in front of me and sat down.

I said : " Where do I go from here ? "

He looked at me and smiled. He said : " Well, there's two things can be done. We can either write Sammy off and let it go like that or you can try somehow to pick up the pieces and see what you can make of it. You and he were rather friendly, weren't you ? "

I said : " Yes, Sammy was rather a friend of mine."

He said : " What a piece of luck that he should have to be killed at a time like this. That's what you'd call a bad break, isn't it ? "

I got up. I said : " It's not so good. I'll be on my way." I smiled at him. " I think we'll take the second alternative," I said. " I'll see if I can put any of the pieces together. There's no harm in trying anyway."

He liked that. He gave me one of his big toothy grins. He said : " You're not a bed feller after all. You're damn conceited, but you're not so bad. You do what you can. If you want anything let me know."

I said I would.

He went on : " If I know anything about you, you're interested in something. Something's got you over this business, hasn't it ? I suppose you were fonder of Carew than you're inclined to let on ? "

I lit a cigarette. " Maybe," I said. " Maybe it's that, but there's another thing. He wasn't killed by any ' doodle ' bomb. *Somebody* killed him."

He raised his eyebrows. He said : " So you think it's like that ? "

I said : " I know it is. I'll be seeing you."

I went out into the street. I left him looking at the glass of port.

After a bit I began to walk back in the direction of Verity Street. Inside I was rather tickled with the whole business. I thought it was one of the funniest spots I had ever been in my life. So Sammy had been on to something that he hadn't told anybody about, but he was going to tell me. And then when he got the chance at the party last night night he ducked. That was probably because he knew he was high and didn't want to talk then. Well, he certainly wouldn't talk now, and the Old Man had put me in a spot—a bad spot. I'd got to play this off the cuff. Whoever 'it was said " when in doubt don't " wasn't really very wise. If you're in doubt and you don't do anything, things get worse. The thing to do is to follow your nose. It's certain to lead you into something some time.

I stood in front of Janine's front door looking at her engraved card under the bell-push, wondering about her. After a bit I stabbed the bell with my forefinger. The door clicked open and I went up the curving stairs. She was standing on the landing leaning against the doorpost in practically the same attitude as when I'd seen her before.

I said : " Hello, Janine ! "

She said shortly : " Well, what is it now ? "

I smiled at her. " You sound tough," I said, " or, alternatively, you make me sound importunate—I think that's the word—importunate—isn't it ? "

She said : " Is it ? I don't think I mind. Did you want to tell me something or ask me something ? "

I said : " You were perfectly right about Sammy Carew. I went round to the mortuary and had a look at him. He looked quite nice. His face wasn't touched at all."

She said : " Yes ? And the rest of him ? "

" The rest of him wasn't so good," I said. " He'd been messed about with considerably, I should say, by the look of it. By the way, I wish you'd tell me something. This policeman who came back to the house and told you that Sammy was dead—did he tell you that *he'd* seen him leave the house, or did he just say that Sammy had *been seen* leaving the house ? "

There was a pause. The silence seemed almost heavy. She asked : " Why ? "

" Look, Janine," I said, " I'm the one who's asking the

17

questions. You'll know all about it some time I've no doubt. Just tell me what I want to know. Did the policeman say he'd seen Sammy leaving the house ? "

She said : " I don't remember exactly what he said. Why should I ? You know, there wasn't any reason why I should be particularly interested in your friend Carew."

I asked : " No ? What was he—just another caller ? "

She flushed a little. She said : " What do you mean by that one ? "

I said : " Whatever you want me to mean. All right. We've decided that you weren't particularly interested in Carew. Now try and remember about the policeman."

She said : " Perhaps I'm not sufficiently interested." Her tone was insolent. " What do you do about it if I don't even want to remember ? "

I looked at her. I said : " You'll remember."

She brought one hand from behind her. There was a cigarette in it. She put it in her mouth and inhaled deeply. Her lips were raspberry colour. She had an almost perfect mouth.

She said : " I don't think the policeman said he'd seen Sammy leaving the house. I think what he said was a gentleman who'd been seen leaving the house had walked across the Square ; had been killed there ; did I know who he was ? "

I nodded. I said : " Thanks a lot, Janine. That was very kind of you."

She said : " All right. I've told you something. Now you tell me something. Why do you ask if Carew was just another caller ? What do you think this is—this flat ? "

I said : " I wouldn't know. But maybe I'll be able to answer your question in a minute. Tell me something, do you know a young man who uses face-powder and something that looks suspiciously like lipstick ; fairly tall, with a thin white face and sleek black hair. Do you ? "

She said : " I can't remember one. Why should I ? "

I said : " He told me not very long ago that he'd seen Carew and you in a public house called The Heap of Feathers this evening ; that he left there with you. Well, of course, that's impossible. Carew was dead by then.

Do you remember that young man ? Have you ever seen him there ? "

She said : " I might have. He's a damned liar anyway. I haven't been in The Heap of Feathers this evening. I don't know what he's talking about."

I said : " Well, if you say that I believe you, but when I asked him for your address here he said everybody knows Janine's address. You wouldn't know what he meant by that ? "

She said : " No."

I said : " All right. Thanks, Janine. I'll be seeing you."

She moved away from the door-post. She said : " Just a minute." Her soft voice had hardened a little. " What is all this ? Who are you ? What are you trying to get at ? "

I said : " Honey, I'm not quite certain at the present moment. I feel rather like Santa Claus in disguise."

I waved my hand to her. " Don't do anything I wouldn't like to hear about," I said.

I began to walk down the stairs. When I was halfway down, she said, in the same tired disinterested voice : " You go to hell, Mr. Whoever-you-are ! " There was something about her voice that intrigued me. I rather liked it. I wondered if I'd see her again. I went out of the front door.

I went home, had a whisky and soda, went into the bedroom, which was a nice cool place, with an atmosphere that I liked, sat down on the bed and began to do a little quiet thinking. One way and another Sammy had put me in a hell of a spot, but I forgave him, not only because he was dead but because everybody always forgave Sammy anything he did. He was that sort of man. There was something about him that sort of reached out and got you, if you know what I mean. By and large I was a little bit steamed up about Sammy.

I had another whisky and soda and began to walk up and down the room. Then I unlocked my suitcase—the one I hadn't unpacked—and took out the Mauser automatic. It was a nice job, as near a .38 as matters, with an S.S. bulbous silencer over the specially shortened barrel. I looked at the clip, put the pistol in my inside breast pocket—the one under my left arm. Then I went out.

I walked around for a bit waiting to see if some idea would descend from Heaven and hit me. It didn't. Darkness was falling and the night wasn't even fresh now. It was oppressive and hot—one of those nights which are inclined to depress you, that is if you're the sort of person who gets depressed over a thing like the atmosphere.

After a bit I walked round to Mulbery Street. I went down the little passageway and looked into the saloon bar of The Heap of Feathers. The bar was crowded but the fancy boy with the white face and black hair was still standing in the corner on the other side of the bar. He seemed to be still working on the crossword puzzle, or perhaps he'd found another one.

I looked at my watch. It was twenty minutes to eleven. I went away and began to walk round the neighbourhood. At the top of Mulbery Street on the left was a narrow turning leading off in a westerly direction. There were two or three empty houses with " to let " boards outside. The street was quiet and deserted. I walked down to the furthest house that was vacant, got my keys out and started work on the front door. I had it open in a couple of minutes. I went inside, shut the door behind me.

It was a pretty big sort of house with a passage that ran from front to rear and a flight of stairs on the left. I switched on my cigarette lighter, walked along the passage, found a door leading to the basement. I went down. It was one of those old-fashioned basements. At the end was a windowless scullery.

The place was unfurnished and dusty. In the corner of the scullery was a packing case with one side knocked out. I went upstairs, out into the street. I left the door unlatched behind me.

I walked back to Mulbery Street. It was three minutes to eleven and people were just beginning to trickle out of the public houses in the street. I stood in a doorway and waited. Just before eleven the boy friend came out of The Heap of Feathers. He had got his newspaper folded under his arm and he stood on the pavement smoothing back his sleek hair. I hoped he'd come my way. He stood for a minute or two, seeming uncertain as to which way he was going ; then he turned and began to saunter towards my end of the street. That pleased me. He moved very slowly and by the time he got opposite me the street was practically deserted. He walked in the middle of the road and when he was nearly opposite me I moved over so that I was just behind him on his left-hand side.

He turned his head, recognised me. He smiled. He said : " I hope you found Janine."

I said : " Yes, thanks. Are you doing anything at the moment ? "

He did not stop walking. He sauntered casually along, looking at me over his shoulder. He had the half-insolent expression on his face that one associates with his type.

He said : " Well, I have an appointment. Is there anything I can do for you ? "

I put my hand inside my coat and brought out the Mauser. I pushed it into his side underneath his left arm.

I said : " Listen, you're going to have a little walk with me. I want to talk to you."

He didn't seem frightened or very surprised. He said : " Very well."

We turned into the narrow street at the top of Mulbery Street, walked down to my empty house. I pushed him in in front of me. I switched on my lighter, pushed him along the passage down the stairs into the basement. I showed him the packing case.

I said : " Go and sit on that. I want to talk to you. And don't move because I shall hear you." I switched off the lighter because there wasn't a lot of petrol in it and I knew I was going to want it. I said : " When did you see Sammy Carew last ? "

I heard him sigh. He said : " I don't know what you're talking about and you're boring me."

I said : " You'd be surprised how much you're going to be bored, bastard."

He said : " Really." I could visualise him raising his arched eyebrows.

21

I said : " So you're not going to talk ? "

He said : " What—to you ? " He called me a very rude name.

I said : " All right. I'll do the talking. You knew that sometime yesterday morning early Carew went to Janine's place. You were very interested. Why ? Perhaps I can make a guess why. You followed him there ; then you hung about. When he came out, you went down Verity Street with him, watched him crossing the Square ; then you heard the flying-bomb come. You weren't in the Square. You probably stood in a doorway. The bomb killed him. So then you went and told the policeman and he went back to Janine's place and told her. That's right, isn't it ? "

He said : " Yes." The word was almost a hiss. " That's right."

I laughed. I said : " You lousy liar. Carew was dead when he was taken and pushed under that truck and somebody had smashed him up pretty good too. They knew that the flying-bomb would be accepted as the cause of death so they wouldn't look for the bullet holes that were in him and which they couldn't possibly find anyhow."

I heard him draw his breath in.

I said : " It was a rule of Sammy Carew's always to have a full clip of ammunition in his automatic. When I went round to the mortuary this evening there were two shells missing, so he'd put up a fight somewhere. I'll find out where.

" All right. When he was dead you carried him over to the excavation place where they're doing the repairs in the Square just on the other side of the gardens. The place was deserted. Maybe you intended to dump him there—you and your friends. Then you had a bit of luck. The bomb came. You got out of the way and it blew the repair truck on top of Carew. It smashed him up in just the way you wanted him smashed up. Well, what about that ? "

He laughed. He said. " I've never seen this man Carew in my life. I think you're mad."

I said : " Maybe. The trouble with people like you is

you're too vain, you know ; so vain that sometimes you forget to be clever." There was a silence ; then I heard a click. I'd heard it before. It is the blade of a long-bladed knife being opened. I snapped on the lighter. He was sitting on the packing-case with a knife lying flat in the palm of his left hand. He was ready to throw it.

I shot him through the stomach. The Mauser made a noise like somebody pulling a cork out of a bottle. He fell over backwards against the wall. I gave him another one through the heart. That finished him. I went over and stood looking at him as he lay slumped in the corner on the other side of the packing-case.

I leaned over, took up his left hand and took Sammy's ring off it—the one I'd tried to file off his finger when he had snake bite in South America. I put it in my pocket.

Then I went over the boy friend. I went through his pockets and over all the " clever " places where clever people hide things. He had nothing on him except the stub of pencil he'd been using on the crossword puzzle.

I tipped him into the packing-case, pushed it up against the wall. I thought it would be a long time before anybody found him.

I lit a cigarette and leaned up against the wall—thinking. It had been an interesting evening. There had been Auntie and Janine and the Old Man and the white-faced person in the packing-case, and it was all very interesting and exciting—if you liked interest and excitement. Personally speaking, I don't. I've had too much of it.

But I'd managed to collect one or two ideas in the course of the evening . . . just one or two.

I stubbed out the cigarette and went upstairs. I opened the front door just a bit and made certain that there was no one in the street ; then I slipped out.

I went home.

CHAPTER TWO

MRS. VAILE

I WOKE UP at six o'clock in the morning. It was hot. I got up and began to walk about the apartment. Four things were predominant in my mind. The first was the little pile of swansdown that I had found in the ebony tray on Sammy's dressing-table. The second was the white-faced young man with whom I had already dealt. The third was Janine and the fourth was Auntie. I thought that these would give me enough to think about for the time being.

And if I wanted anything additional there was the incongruity of the stories told me by the white-faced boyo and Janine. I wondered why he had been careful to tell me when I first met him in the bar at The Heap of Feathers that Sammy had gone off with Janine that evening. Why had he told me this? Surely he would guess that, as I was looking for Sammy, I would go immediately to Janine's address. Surely he realised that she would throw down his story? Or had he, *at that time*, reason to believe that she would support it?

Anyhow, she had *not* supported it. On the contrary she had told what appeared, on the face of it, to be the truth. I mentally shrugged my shoulders. This was just another of those things. You could think about it as much as you liked, but the process wouldn't get you anywhere.

I walked about from one room to another for an hour and a half. Most of the time I was being sentimental. I was thinking about the old days in South America—and one or two other places. Of course all days are good in retrospect, but there had been a certain atmosphere—a colour—about those times which was lacking in these days.

A damned silly idea this, of course. One's own job always seems prosaic, no matter what it may be, and what

24

is exciting to one person is merely boring to another. I realised that I wasn't bored—on the contrary, I was worried, but was not too keen on admitting the fact. Incidentally—although he was no longer with us—I was not so pleased with Sammy. He'd played it badly. He'd gone out of this job and left no indications at all—which, believe it or not, was not like Sammy.

Soon after eight I had a cold shower, rang for breakfast, and dressed. By this time I'd definitely come to the conclusion that the only way to play this business was to do it like a bull in a china shop—just go right ahead and take a smash at everything that got in the way. This process can be damned interesting—specially if somebody takes a smash at you first.

At nine o'clock I telephoned the Old Man at his private number. When he came on the line he was as sweet as a dove.

He said : " Well, young feller . . . what is it now ? "

" I'll tell you," I said. " I've done some thinking and I've got a series of ideas which may or may not come off. Anyway, there's no harm in trying. I want some help."

" Well, that's all right," he said. " What sort of help do you want ? "

I said : " I don't quite know, but if you've got anybody who is good and tough and intelligent—but especially tough—I'd like somebody like that. And I'd like a woman—not too old and not too young. Old enough to have sense and poise and intelligence, and young enough to have charm, just in case she has to use it on somebody. Can you do anything about that ? "

He grunted. " All right. You can consider it done. I'll send them round to you. When ? "

I thought for a moment. Then : " Well, I'm going to give myself a day off. I'm going to do a little walking round a golf course. I find I think easier on a golf course. I'm coming back to London this afternoon. I'd like to see the man about six. I'll see him here at this place, and the woman had better meet me at the Gay Sixties Club at nine."

" All right," said the Old Man. " Is that all ? "

I said : " Yes . . . thank you very much."

I heard the receiver click. He was never one for wasting words.

I walked around for a bit and at half-past ten I went round to the garage, got out the car, drove down to Surrey. I like the country round there. I ambled through Dorking and pulled the car up in a cutting by the Betchworth Golf Course about a mile outside the town.

I got out of the car and began to wander over the course. I'm very fond of that course. The year the war started I'd played there quite a lot with Sammy, and walking down towards the ninth hole by the avenue of limes I remembered some of the jokes and wisecracks he'd pulled in those days. It was a lovely morning. The sun was shining and there was a little breeze.

I sat down on the little hillock by the dog-leg turn at the twelfth. This place had always been a favourite spot of mine. I lit a cigarette and for some reason began to think of the night when Sammy and I had run into a bunch of trouble at Fourelles in the Pas de Calais. I remembered Sammy coming out of the rocket assembly hut with the rather high collar of his Oberlieutenant of Artillery jacket undone, bleeding like a stuck pig from a gash in the cheek. When I got into the hut I found a young Maquisard lying in the corner unconscious. Sammy had been forced to knock him out after the other fellow had tried first of all to strangle him and then to stab him. I suppose the young Frenchman had wanted to wreck the assembly plant. They were very keen on doing that sort of thing in those days.

I can remember Sammy cursing and swearing like a trooper ; calling the Maquis and the English Secret Service—the Pas de Calais Cloak and Dagger Brigade we used to call them—every name under the sun. Eventually we got the Maquis on to a cart under a pile of fresh dung—which Sammy said would teach him something when he came to—and carted him off. Definitely, I thought, *those* were the days.

I turned my head and looked towards the twelfth tee. A woman was coming round the corner, passing the tee and coming down the middle of the fairway. A peach. About thirty-two or three, I should say ; slim and very well-figured, with good ankles and a swing to her walk. She was a brunette, looked a lady, and was wearing a grey flannel coat and skirt with a chalk stripe, a grey pull-on felt hat and trim suede walking shoes.

As she came towards me—she was walking by the rough edge of the fairway on the opposite side to my hillock—I got one of my funnier ideas. I suppose it was rather clutching at a straw but I was in that sort of frame of mind. Anyway, I made up my mind to try it. In any event it would be an interesting experiment.

As she came to within about twenty yards of me I got up and stepped clumsily over the hillock. I fell over, picked myself up and then let out a sharp exclamation and stood, perched on one leg, like a stork, with an expression of intense agony on my face.

She fell for it. She came over. She said : " Is there anything wrong ? Are you hurt ? "

I sat down on the side of the hillock. I said : " I'm afraid I am. I've twisted my ankle badly. I trod on a loose stone or something."

She looked at me with a pair of attractive brown eyes. Her gaze was quite steady yet somehow casual. I felt that this woman possessed some peculiar power of attraction that I could not explain.

She said, with a smile : " I'm sorry about that. But that's what happens to people who go mooning about golf courses. Anyway, this Club is reserved for members."

I said : " How do you know I'm not a member ? "

She said : " Well, you may be but I've never seen you before."

I said : " Well, I am a member and for that matter I've never seen *you* before. Incidentally, you're going to have to do something about me."

She sat down on the other end of the hillock. She had *very* good ankles.

She said : " Exactly what do you mean by that, sir ? "

I said : " Well, I don't think I can walk on my left foot. You see, I've twisted this ankle so many times it's becoming rather a dangerous proposition. I shall have to get to a doctor somehow."

She sighed and produced a cigarette case. She took a cigarette, handed the case to me. I lit the cigarettes.

She said : " You don't look the sort of man who would be such a nuisance."

I looked at her. I said : " I'm sorry to be a nuisance but I can't help myself. The thing is that I shall have to get to a doctor. I think I've put one of the small bones out. I've done it before and it can easily be put right. The thing is getting to a doctor."

She smiled. When she smiled she looked quite delightful. She said : " And how do we do that ? "

So she was going to play ! " That's easy," I said. " If you'll lend me your stick I'll manage to hobble back to my car. But I don't think I can drive it. I couldn't use this foot on the clutch."

She asked where the car was. I told her.

She said : " Well, we can make it much simpler than that. If you just walk across the course through the rough and through the gate, you'll come on to the road. If you give me the car key I'll drive it up. I can pick you up there. Then we can go and get your foot seen to. Incidentally, I'm sorry about your foot."

I grinned at her. " If I *have* to put a bone out in my ankle on a golf course," I said, " I shall always prefer to do it when there is a delightful, not to say lovely, person like yourself in the vicinity."

She raised her eyebrows. " Well . . . well . . ." she said. " I take that speech in the spirit in which I hope it was meant. By the way, who are you ? "

I told her my name was Kells.

She said : " I am Mrs. Vaile." She handed me her walking stick and I began to hobble across the fairway. She came with me to the other side in case I fell over. Once on the path I gave her the car key and she went off. I watched her walking back towards the twelfth tee. I liked the way she walked.

I thought to myself : This is a hell of a dirty trick to play on a nice woman. But what the hell could I do anyway. I had to get started somehow.

I hobbled along the path towards the road.

We stopped outside a doctor's house on the outskirts of Dorking. It took us only a few minutes to get there but during those few minutes neither of us spoke. Once or twice I thought she gave me a quick sidelong glance— the sort of look a woman gives if she is at all interested in a man—but this might have been my fancy. She drove a car well ; she was deft and nimble in handling the wheel. Altogether, having regard to what was in my mind, I was sorry for her.

The doctor was at home and I hobbled inside and spent ten minutes talking to him about all sorts of things, doing anything I could to waste time. When I came out my hobble was still pronounced but not quite so obvious.

She asked : " Well ? "

I said : " It's not quite so bad as I thought. The ankle's badly sprained but nothing's broken. It's tied up and it should be all right in a few days—at least that's what the doctor says."

She said : " I'm very glad to hear it. I was getting a little worried about you."

I looked at her sideways. Her eyes were mischievous.

I said : " I'm glad to hear that because I've got to get back to London and I can't drive this car. What are we going to do about that one ? "

She said : " Well, that's not difficult. I was going back to town this afternoon anyway. I'll drive you back."

" That's wonderful," I answered. " But you're sure I'm not putting you to any inconvenience ? "

She said airily : " Oh no. I never do anything I don't want to do."

I grinned at her. " Well, Mrs. Vaile, you're a very lucky woman," I said. I was wondering to myself what she'd think if she knew what was in my mind.

On the way back we talked about the sweet nothings that one usually does talk about on these occasions.

When she stopped the car outside my apartments she said : " Is there somebody who can take this car round to the garage for you or shall I do it ? "

I said : " You needn't bother to do that. My foot's feeling a lot better and I've an idea that I shall be able to use it more or less normally in a few hours. Besides, the porter here can take the car away."

She said : " All right. Perhaps your porter can get me a cab."

I said : " In a minute. But this isn't quite satisfactory, is it ? "

She looked at me with her eyebrows raised. She said : " What do you mean by that ? "

I grinned at her.

I said : " You ought to know that *you* were the cause of my spraining my ankle. . . ."

She looked very astonished. She asked : " Whatever *do* you mean ? "

I shrugged my shoulders. " You know how it is," I said. I looked straight into her eyes and smiled at her. I put every goddamned thing I've got into that smile. " Every man has an ideal woman in his head. You know what I mean—a sort of mental picture that he carries about with him. But he never expects actually to meet the lady. Well . . . I did. And when I saw you and realised that you were the woman I'd been thinking about for years I got a little excited and fell over. So you must admit you owe me something. . . ."

She asked casually : " Such as ? "

I said : " Well, I think you ought to dine with me to-night. I'm feeling rather lonely. What do you think about that ? "

She said : " You've got your nerve, haven't you ? In point of fact the idea rather appeals to me. Where shall we dine ? "

I said : " I think it would be a very good idea if you met me at the Berkeley at a quarter-past nine. I promise you a very good dinner."

She said slowly : " Well, I ought not to do it, but I'm going to. You're an interesting type, aren't you, Mr. Kells ? "

I said : " You'd be surprised. So that's a bet—nine-fifteen at the Berkeley ? "

She nodded. " I'll be there. Thank you very much."

I went inside, got the porter to get a cab, and she went off. I watched the cab go down the street. I thought : Well, it's tough but it's got to be done. For the business I had in mind she would do as well as anybody else.

At six o'clock the porter rang through to my apartment. He told me that there was a gentleman to see me. I told him to send him up. I liked the look of him when he came into the room. He was a thin, youngish type of man, going a little bald on top. He had a very intelligent face and a good jaw.

I said : " Good-afternoon. What's your name ? "

He told me his name was Charles Freeby ; that the Old Man had told him to see me at six o'clock.

I gave him a whisky and soda, told him to sit down and asked him what sort of work he had been doing. He told me. He seemed to have a pretty varied background.

" Well, so long as you haven't got a queasy stomach you'll be all right on this job," I said, " although I think I ought to tell you it's liable to be a little tough."

He smiled. He said : " I don't think I mind that."

I thought he would do. He wasn't noticeable—you'd never see him in a crowd. There was a peculiar sense of urgency about him. It struck me that he was the type of man who wouldn't waste any time. I put his age at about thirty and thought that he was probably much stronger than he looked—one of those thin wiry people.

When he'd finished his drink he said : " What's the first move ? "

I asked him if the Old Man had told him anything about me.

He smiled. He said he'd told him quite a bit about me, but nothing about the work he was to do.

I said : " He couldn't have told you that because he doesn't know. Neither do I."

He grinned. He said : " That makes it sound interesting."

I told him it probably would be before it was through. I gave him a cigarette and lit one for myself.

I said : " Look . . . to-night at nine-fifteen I'm going to have dinner with a woman at the Berkeley. She's about five feet eight inches—a very good slim figure, good feet and ankles. She has brown eyes and reddish brown hair and a rather curly humorous sort of mouth. She's a Mrs. Vaile. You've got all that ? "

He said he'd got it.

" When we've had dinner she'll go off," I went on. " I don't know where she's going to or how she proposes to get there. She might have a car ; she might send for a cab ; she might walk. But I want you to go after her. Stick close to her—see what happens. If nothing happens to-night try and pick her up to-morrow morning."

He asked : " This job looks like an indefinite one. How long do I keep on tailing her ? "

" Until something happens," I said.

He said : " And you think something's going to happen ? "

I nodded.

" Such as ? " he queried.

" I couldn't tell you," I said. " But somebody might try to start something. Somebody might try to be tough with this woman. They might."

" I see," he said. " And you want her kept all in one piece ? "

" That's right," I said. " I'm sorry it's so vague but that's the way it is."

He said that was all right. He finished his drink, picked up his hat and went away. I rather liked him.

I had a cocktail and read the newspapers. The news was fairly good. It looked as if with some luck the war in Europe might be over in a year. I hoped it would be. I'm sick of wars, mainly because they don't allow my peculiar characteristics to develop, or maybe they allow them to develop too much. I'm not quite certain which.

When I'd finished I walked round to Kinnoul Street. I stood looking at No. 23 wondering why Sammy had elected to stay there. Sammy always stayed in an hotel. He liked hotels. He loathed furnished rooms.

I pressed the bell and waited. Nothing happened. No one ever seemed to be in at No. 23. I gave the door a push, and sure enough it opened. I thought Auntie must be a very trusting person.

I went into the hall, shut the door behind me and called out : " Auntie ! " Nothing happened. I walked up the stairs and went into Sammy's room. The place had been cleaned and dusted. Two suitcases which I recognised as Sammy's were on the luggage stand at the bottom of the bed and his clothes and belongings neatly arranged were stacked on the bed.

I lit a cigarette, walked over and began to look through them. I looked into the coats ; noticed that the linings had been badly sewn in. That was odd having regard to the meticulous care which Sammy bestowed on his clothes. Anyhow I probably guessed about that.

I went upstairs and had a look in some of the other rooms. They were nicely furnished. In the larger room on the floor above Sammy's was a framed picture of Auntie on the mantelpiece. I thought Auntie was a nice-looking woman, but I wished I could find her in some-time. I wondered who did the work in the house.

I came down the stairs, closed Sammy's bedroom door, went downstairs and wandered through the rooms on the ground floor. They were all empty. Then I went out of the house. But I shut the door behind me. I thought that Auntie ought not to be so trusting. Incidentally, I hoped she'd got a key. Maybe she hadn't. Perhaps it wasn't her house. I grinned to myself. How should I know ?

I arrived at the Gay Sixties at five minutes to nine ; stood on the other side of the street watching the people go in. After a few minutes a well-dressed girl whom I thought would probably be the one I was looking for came up from the direction of Berkeley Square and entered the Club. She was of middle height, slim, and carried her-self with an air.

I walked over, went into the Club. She was at the end of the bar, drinking a gin and lime.

I went along to her. I said : " Good-evening. Would you by any chance be looking for me ? "

She smiled. She was pretty in a poised sort of way, and had the peculiar sophisticated look that most women who work in our racket acquire.

She said : " I think so. You're Mr. Kells, aren't you ? "

I said : " That's right. Who sent you to meet me ? "

She told me. I ordered myself a whisky and soda, and another gin and lime for her.

I said : " I haven't a great deal of time to talk. This is the thing. Not very far away there's a street called Verity Street. At No. 16, in the first floor apartment, is a woman who calls herself Janine—rather attractive. I don't know very much about her and I'd like to. I want to know when she went there, what she does for a living ; anything you can pick up. Perhaps one of the other tenants could be got at."

I gave her a slip of paper with my telephone number and address on it. " Learn that off," I said, " then throw it away. When you've got anything to tell me ring me up. By the way, what's your name ? "

She said her name was Alison Fredericks ; that she understood exactly what I wanted her to do. She said she'd call through as soon as she'd got something. She looked an efficient sort of girl, but then the Old Man never used anybody who wasn't. She finished her drink and got up.

She said : " Well . . . I'll go to work." She hesitated for a moment then : " I suppose this is one of those things where one has to be careful ? "

I smiled at her. " You'd be surprised how careful you've got to be," I said. " Don't stick your neck out, will you ? "

She made a little moue. " No, Mr. Kells, I won't," she said. " By the way, I'd like you to know how fearfully pleased I am at being allowed to work for you. I think it's great fun."

I didn't say anything. I hoped it was going to be great fun too—but I had my doubts.

When she had gone I bought another whisky and soda. Then I walked up the road to the Berkeley. I had only been there a couple of minutes when Mrs. Vaile appeared.

I took a long look at her as she came across the lounge. She was charmingly dressed. She looked delightful and had an attractive air of vitality.

She sat down and I ordered her a drink ; gave her a cigarette. When the waiter had gone she said : " Mr. Kells, I ought to tell you that you intrigue me. But you probably know that. You guessed that I'd dine with you to-night in order to satisfy my curioisty. I think you're rather a tiresome person."

I said : " I'm very pleased to hear that I intrigue you. Any man would be happy to intrigue a woman as beautiful as you are . . . and as intelligent." I grinned at her.

She made a clicking noise with her tongue. " You ought to know." she went on, " that I believe that stuff about your ankle was pure fiction. I was rather dubious about it from the start. So, to-night, I stopped my cab on the other side of the road a good ten minutes ago and watched you walk up from the Gay Sixties. There's nothing at all the matter with your ankle."

I shrugged my shoulders. " My powers of recuperation *are* rather good," I said. " But even if my ankle is fairly well I'm beginning to develop a peculiar form of heart attack that doesn't please me at all."

We went into dinner. We ate an excellent meal and talked a great deal about nothing at all. In ten minutes we were calling each other by our Christian names. I must say I found her very interesting to listen to. She had a unique phraseology—a quick and humorous mentality. Also, now that I'd had an opportunity to look at her at really close quarters, I could see that she was an extremely attractive woman. Her eyes were bright and peculiarly luminous. Her voice was soft and there was an odd and indefinable allure about her.

When we were drinking our coffee I discovered, with a start, that I was beginning to think that I was a bit of a so-and-so to be making use of this woman ; that I might easily be putting her in a spot that was very dangerous. I smiled inwardly. The idea of *me* considering anything or anybody except the job in hand was amusing. In a minute, I told myself, I should be falling in love ! I must say the idea was funny. I wondered what the hell the Old Man would say about that !

She went at ten-fifteen. The doorman got her a cab and I stood on the pavement outside the Berkeley with my foot on the running board looking at her through the open window. We looked at each other for quite a bit.

She said, suddenly and rather breathlessly, I thought : " You're a bit of a bastard, aren't you, Michael dear ? Just a little bit ? "

I registered surprise. " I'm shocked," I told her. " I've never heard such a sweet mouth use such a wicked word. Still, you *were* smiling when you said it. But why am I a bit of a bastard ? "

She made a little grimace. She said : " You knew perfectly well, from the start, that if I came to dine with you I was at any rate a *little* bit interested in you. So you carefully tell me nothing at all about yourself. You've evaded most cleverly, every question I've asked. Having done nothing about satisfying my curiosity you propose to let me go without even asking if you could see me again. I'm fearfully disappointed in you, Michael. For a man who *looks* so intriguing . . ."

I said : " Listen, Bettina, I had a very good reason for not asking you if I might see you again. In fact I was perfectly certain that if I didn't, you'd do it without being asked." I gave her my most impertinent grin.

She sighed heavily. " The damned insolence of the man," she said. " Well . . . you'll find my address in the telephone book. Come and have a drink one evening . . . about six-thirty."

I said : " That's very kind of you, Bettina."

" Not at all," she said primly. " But I still want to satisfy my curiosity and I intend to do it."

I said : " I think you're a sweet, Bettina. I think you ought to know that I go for you in a very big way indeed. In fact, if this car weren't blocking up the whole of the Berkeley entrance I'd tell you one or two things I think about you. I'd tell you about your eyes and the delightful way you talk and . . . well *you* know."

She sighed again. " You're not only intriguing, you're damned dangerous, Michael," she said. " You've said those very words to a hundred women. Oh dear . . . why do I always become interested in men like that . . . Well . . . good-night, Michael dear . . . come and see me.''

The cab went off towards Berkeley Square. Halfway down the street, I saw Freeby, in a little black two-seater, pull out from the pavement and go after it. So that was all right.

I lit a cigarette and began to walk down Piccadilly towards my flat.

The telephone rang at about one o'clock in the morning. I sat up in bed with a start and grabbed the receiver. It was Freeby.

He said : '' You were right about your girl friend. She went to a house in Charles Street first of all. Luckily I saw the cab slow down and was able to pull round the side turning. I'm glad about that. There was another taxi on her tail. A man got out—a thin man, rather tall. He paid it off ; looked up and down the street ; parked himself in a porch on the other side of the road. He was there two or three minutes ; then another taxicab came up from the direction of Berkeley Square and stopped just near where he was waiting. Somebody got out and he got in. But the cab stayed there. When your friend came out of the house she got into a taxi that had apparently been telephoned for. When it went off, the cab on the other side of the road went after it.

'' She went on to a rather swell bottle party. The man went off in the cab, and about fifteen minutes later— they'd evidently taken a chance on her staying that length of time—a little two-seater coupé came up. It was driven by a woman—middle-aged, rather attractive. When Mrs. Vaile came out of the bottle party about three quarters of an hour later, the woman in the two-seater went after her ; tailed her home. When she'd seen her home she went off. That's all I know.''

I said : '' All right, Freeby. You pick up Mrs. Vaile to-morrow morning. Ring me again when you've got something.''

He said good-night and rang off. I hung up the receiver, lay back in bed, considered the situation. So I'd been right in my guess that our friends would put a tail on Mrs. Vaile. It was obvious to me that they were very curious about anyone I knew. It was obvious that they were wise to me, just as it had seemed they had been wise to Sammy. It rather looked as if they were going to take a very great interest in me and in people seen with me. It seemed quite possible that they were going to take as deep an interest in us as they had in Sammy, but I hoped not with the same results.

I got up, dressed. I was feeling a little bored. I suppose in a way I like excitement but I do like to know exactly what I'm doing. The uncertainty of this business was annoying me.

I walked slowly round to Kinnoul Street, rang the bell. I wondered if anybody was going to open the door *this* time. I waited two or three minutes ; then the door was opened. Auntie, looking very nice in a black and grey silk dressing-gown, stood in the hallway.

I said : " Good-morning, Auntie. How are you ? "

She shrugged her shoulders. " I'll be damned," she said. She smiled at me. " It's that man again. What the so-and-so do you want *now*—and at this time in the morning. I suppose you're still looking for Sammy ? "

I said : " No, I've given it up. Sammy's dead."

She said : " My God ! " She stepped back into the hallway. She said : " You'd better come in."

I went in. She opened the door of the room on the right of the hall. It was evidently a dining room. Quite obviously, I had interrupted her in the middle of a late supper.

She said : " If you'd like to eat something, sit down. There's whisky on the sideboard."

I said : " Thanks, I'll have a drink."

She sat down at the table. She said : " What's all this about Sammy ? You're not being funny or anything, are you ? "

I said : " It's not the sort of thing one would be funny about, is it ? "

She said : " Well, you never know. Some people have a strange sense of humour. Tell me about it."

I said : " It's quite simple. Apparently Sammy went to a public house called The Heap of Feathers, and after that went off somewhere else. Anyway, he was seen crossing the Square near Mulbery Street. Just at that moment a ' doodle-bug ' came down and that was the end of Sammy."

She said : " Are you quite certain ? "

I nodded. " I went to the mortuary and saw him," I said. " It was Sammy all right. Incidentally, they'd like you to go round. I told them you were his nearest relative. Perhaps you'd like me to take you round in the morning."

She said : " No, I needn't trouble you. I'll go round on my own."

I said : " All right. If you prefer it."

She said : " It's a pretty awful thing, isn't it ? I was very fond of Sammy."

I said : " Yes, I've gathered that was so." I finished my whisky and soda. I said : " Well, it's been nice meeting you, Auntie. I'll be on my way."

She looked at me sombrely. She said : " Don't go. Have another drink. I'd like to talk to you."

I poured myself out another whisky and soda.

She said suddenly : " What's your name ? "

I told her my name was Kells.

She said : " I take it you knew Sammy pretty well, didn't you ? "

I said : " Yes . . . I knew Sammy pretty well. We were rather friendly—at least we were when we weren't quarrelling about some woman or other."

She nodded. " You'd be like that—you two," she said. Her expression was very gloomy. " Sammy was a fine, good-looking and intelligent type that women liked, and you—well—you've got something. You look a little like George Raft to me. Anyhow, I suppose women would like you too. I can imagine you two rowing all the time about some worthless piece just because you hadn't anything better to think about."

I didn't say anything.

After a bit she asked : " Did you know what Sammy was doing ? "

I said : " Yes, I know what he was doing."

" What ? " she asked. " Or is it a very great secret ? I know that he was a mysterious boy. Always up to something. Always coming and going and nobody knowing when or where . . . But perhaps you'd rather not tell me. Perhaps it's a great secret—something better left untold —is it ? "

I looked at her. I grinned. I said : " *You* ought to know, Auntie ! "

She asked quickly : " What the deuce do you mean by that ? "

I said : " Listen . . . what is all this ? What sort of damn fool do you think I am ? "

She stiffened. She said : " I don't understand."

" No ? " I said. " You didn't arrange that heap of swansdown in the ebony bowl, did you ? Of course you did. You did it for my benefit. The idea was that I should think that Sammy had left it ; that he wanted to put me on to some place that had to do with feathers. You knew I'd ask you about that. That enabled you apparently quite innocently to put me on to The Heap of Feathers.

" Well, that fancy white-faced boy friend of yours was waiting to put me on to Janine. But something went wrong there. Quite obviously, I wasn't supposed to meet Janine. Perhaps she was supposed to clear out first. And she didn't do it. Anyway, by this time I was pretty good and suspicious. So what do you think I did ? "

She said in a brittle sort of voice : " I don't know. You're talking rubbish. But what *did* you do ? "

I said : " Well, I went round and had a look at Sammy and made certain it was him. I came to the conclusion that somebody had been rather rough with him. It might have been you."

She frowned at me : " What the devil do you mean by that ? " Her voice was almost harsh.

I said : " It might easily be that Sammy was killed here. Anyhow, he took a couple of pot shots at somebody some time before he died. My next idea is that you intended to dump him in that section in the Square where the repair party is at work. They'd been filling in a big bomb hole and it would be the easiest thing in the world 'o dump him there and cover him over. There was no night-watchman and all the tools you wanted. The chances are that he'd never have been seen or heard of again. A very nice job—from *your* point of view. But you had even better luck. My guess is that just when you got him there—you'd probably used the repair party hand-cart—you heard the doodle-bug coming and you all ducked out of the way. You left Sammy. And the blast blew the heavy tractor wagon right on top of him. Knocked him about to such an extent that nobody would ever have known what he'd died of. His body was practically flat. Then you came back and had a look—probably there were three of you, if not more—and you decided to leave him just where he was. Just another flying-bomb casualty. After which somebody wanders off and tells the War Reserve policeman that he believes someone's been killed in the Square. A nice job. A piece of cake. Money for old rope. Congratulations, Auntie ! "

She laughed out loud. " You damned idiot," she said. " You must be mad. You make me laugh. And how do you know all this funny business ? Or did you just make it up as you went along ? "

I thought it was time I tried a couple of flat-footed ones on Auntie.

I said : " I'm going to make you laugh before I'm through, Auntie, and I'm quite prepared to tell you how I know. After I'd seen Sammy I went back and saw your white-faced boy friend. He'd made one very bad mistake. He'd taken Sammy's signet ring off. He probably fancied it. I recognised it. Well, I *made* him talk. He talked a lot. Then I came round here and paid a little visit. In point of fact, I wanted to see you, but the place was empty. I went upstairs and had a look at Sammy's clothes. You'd taken an awful lot of trouble taking the linings out of his coats to see if he'd anything hidden inside . . . hadn't you ? And you sewed the linings in afterwards quite well, but not well enough. I suppose you had to make a quick job of it. Well . . . Auntie ? "

I drew my chair a little nearer to her. " Your only chance is to talk," I said. " Otherwise it's going to be *very* tough for you. And if you don't talk willingly I'm going to make you talk. I'm rather angry with you . . . you lying old bitch ! "

She shrugged her shoulders. She said : " Well . . . I suppose the best thing . . ."

In a flash she had picked up the pepper pot from the table, pulled the top off and let me have the contents in my eyes. If you've never had pepper in your eyes you don't know what life is. By the time I'd got myself into a condition to do anything at all, Auntie was gone, the lights were out and I was left alone in my glory.

I sat there with my eyes streaming, smoking a cigarette. I talked slowly and systematically to myself about Auntie. The things that I called that blue-eyed, quick-fingered hellion were just nobody's business.

I damned her to hell and glory in four different languages.

Then I went home.

CHAPTER THREE

JANINE

It was eleven o'clock when I got out of bed. I went into the bathroom and looked at my eyes. They were still red and inflamed. I put in some heavy work with some boracic lotion, interrupted by a few quiet remarks about Auntie.

I was beginning to be very interested in Auntie. I couldn't understand the set-up at all about that lady. First of all I wondered why Sammy had elected to stay in her house—if it *was* her house. I wondered whether Sammy was wise to Auntie or if she had taken him for a ride. Not knowing what was in Sammy's mind at the time of his death I couldn't say. But I would have liked to have had an idea.

I didn't see that there was any point in thinking about it. I bathed, shaved, put on some clean pyjamas and a dressing-gown, rang for coffee ; began to walk about the apartment trying to think things out.

I came to the conclusion that the difference between what is usually called a detective story and the things that happen in real life is that in the novel there is some sort of pattern of events predestined to fit in to each other. A jigsaw which must have a definite solution because the pieces will only fit into certain sections. But life isn't like that. Anything can happen, and it does. But it happens without any sort of cohesion, and it is more by luck than cleverness that one stumbles on a fact that matters.

I lit my first cigarette of the day and began to think of three people that I was beginning to associate in my mind—Auntie, the white-faced young man, with whom I had dealt, and Janine. At first thought there was some connection between these people. One would have imagined they were working together. After all, it was Auntie who'd put me on to The Heap of Feathers where I'd met the white-faced boy, and it was he who'd put me on to Janine. But there was a snag about this. First of all the information he had given me about Janine and Sammy was *deliberately* incorrect. Secondly, he had tried to get me up against Janine from the start. He'd gone out of his way to suggest that she was no better than she should be. What was his reason for that? I thought I could make a guess about that one. He knew perfectly well that when I left The Heap of Feathers I'd go straight round to Janine's place. He knew that I should tell her that I had information that she and Sammy had left The Heap of Feathers an hour or so before. He knew that she was going to deny this and tell me the story she had told me about Sammy having left early that morning; having been filled by the flying-bomb.

But he thought I wouldn't believe her. He thought I wouldn't believe her because he hoped I'd already put Janine in my mind as a person who was no better than she should be. This might have been quite true, of course, but still she *had* been speaking the truth more or less.

But what was in his mind was obvious. He wanted to plant the idea in my brain that she was lying; that Sammy had gone back with her from The Heap of

Feathers an hour or so before. In other words, when Sammy disappeared I was going to get the idea into my head that she was the last person who'd been with him. Altogether, the white-faced young man wasn't such a fool—although his brains hadn't got him anywhere except in the packing-case where I hoped sincerely he still quietly reposed.

Thinking about this made me inclined to believe that the proverb that there is no honour amongst thieves is a very true one. It seemed to me that my first idea about Auntie, the white-faced person and Janine working together might have been true, but it also appeared that they'd fallen out about something. The most obvious thing for them to fall out about was Sammy's death. Possibly, after Sammy had been finished off, somebody had got scared. Possibly Auntie and White-Face had agreed between themselves to pass the buck as far as was possible to Janine. Well, I thought it might be funny if I played it from their angle. I thought the time had come when I ought to have another interview with Janine.

I switched my mind over to her. Rather an extraordinary person, I thought. One of those rather indefinable people—indefinable because she wanted to appear so. Janine might be anything. She might be a tart, as White-Face had suggested she was, or she might not. I wasn't worrying about those angles particularly, because I was relying on Alison Fredericks to clear all those points up, and I hoped she'd do it quickly.

I hung around the flat until one o'clock. Then I dressed, went out to lunch. I came back afterwards, read a couple of chapters of a book, found that I wasn't taking a particular interest in it, discovered that for some reason which I could not explain I was thinking about Bettina Vaile. Life, I thought, is rather extraordinary when you come to think about it. Here was a woman—an extraordinarily attractive and charming woman—who, because she happened to be taking a walk on a golf course at a time when I was there, was going to find herself embroiled in a very nasty business. I've already said that whilst we were dining at the Berkeley I had a spasm of self-accusation about this business. But you can't make omelettes without breaking eggs. Somebody has to get hurt.

At the same time I wasn't too keen on the idea of Bettina getting hurt. She was much too nice a person. But it was too late for me to do anything about that. All I could do was to hope for the best.

At five o'clock I gave myself a whisky and soda and the telephone bell jangled. It was Alison Fredericks. She said in her cool cheerful voice :

" Good-evening, Mr. Kells. A few minutes ago I left a sealed envelope with the porter at your apartments. He said he'd deliver it to you. I wanted to know that you'd received it safely."

I said : " Just a minute. Someone's at the door now. Hold on."

I went to the door. It was the porter with the envelope. I went back to the telephone. I said :

" I've got it. Is there anything else ? "

She said : " I've told you all I could. I'm still working. I thought you'd like to have something to get on with."

" Good girl," I said. " I'll read this. If you get anything else, no matter whether it seems important or unimportant, ring through."

She said she would and hung up.

I opened the sealed envelope. Inside was a sheet of quarto notepaper neatly typed. It said :

JANINE.

Janine arrived at the house in Verity Street only two days ago. She was wearing an expensive tailormade. The taxi that brought her seemed to carry a considerable amount of luggage, but she took only two suitcases into No. 16. The rest of the stuff was sent away. Since she's been there two or three men have called. I couldn't get a description of them except in the case of one who was described as being very good-looking and rather whimsical. (That would be Sammy all right.)

She makes her own coffee in the morning ; she missed lunch yesterday, but to-day she went out for it. Each night she has dined out. Her clothes are apparently very good and such pieces of jewellery as the woman who runs the place has seen are, she thinks, valuable.

Yesterday afternoon a series of events, which on the face of it seemed a little peculiar, took place. Apparently the woman who keeps the house had been out and was returning. As she approached the house she saw Janine looking through the drawn curtain of her bedroom window down the street. Quite obviously she was looking at a woman of about forty—quite well-dressed, with rather startling blue eyes—who was coming down the street on the opposite side. This woman crossed to No. 16, pressed the Janine bell button, and when the door opened went in. The woman followed her two or three minutes afterwards and went to her own rooms. Quite naturally she believed that the visitor had seen Janine in her rooms, but in this idea she was mistaken because some ten minutes afterwards the blue-eyed woman came downstairs and asked where Janine was.

The landlady said the only explanation was that Janine, wishing to avoid her caller, had gone into the bathroom and stayed there whilst the blue-eyed person waited. The visitor then went away. Some twenty minutes later Janine arrived at the house in a cab, and the woman realised that her theory about Janine having hidden herself in the bathroom was wrong ; that, trying to avoid her visitor, she had obviously gone out of the back door.

The ladylady doesn't seem to know quite what to think about Janine. She likes her. She says she is charming and has good manners, but seems a little bit suspicious of what she describes as ' this funny business.'

I have got one or two more angles on which I propose to work, and I hope to get in touch with you again to-morrow. My telephone number is Sloane 77999.

                                         A.F.

I read Alison's report through twice ; then burned it. It didn't tell me a great deal. I wondered who the men who'd called on Janine were. Obviously one of them was Sammy. It was also obvious to me that the blue-eyed woman of about forty years of age whom Janine had taken such trouble to avoid was Auntie. Janine had seen Auntie coming down the street ; had slipped out of the back door and gone off for three quarters of an hour until the coast was clear and she could return. Why ?

I began to think that I might be right in my supposition that there'd been trouble between this trio. Here is the late White-Face trying to put Janine in bad with me, and Janine doing her best to avoid Auntie.

Somehow this first vague report from Alison gave me a feeling of relief. I had an idea that I was going to get some place. I had another whisky and soda on the strength of it.

After I'd finished my whisky I made a plan for the evening. I thought it would be a good idea to have a drink with Bettina. I looked up her number in the telephone book and called through.

The maid answered the telephone. I told her who I was. A minute later Bettins came on the line. She said : "Good-afternoon, Michael. I'm very glad that you rang through."

I said : "Why is that, Bettina ? Is it because of my fatal attraction or what ? "

She said : "Well, on this particular occasion it is not because of your fatal attraction. Believe it or not, my dear, there are some rather funny things going on around here."

I said : "You don't say so. What sort of things ? And why should they have anything to do with me ? "

"That's the point," she said. "You know, I'm getting more doubtful about you every minute."

I said : "Nonsense, Bettina. You're getting nerves or something. Why should you be doubtful about me ? "

She laughed. "Why shouldn't I ? " she said. "I don't know anything about you. I think you're much too attractive—almost too good to be true. You're too smooth. Too knowledgeable. You've had much too much experience of women. You told me a lot of nonsense about your ankle on the golf course. You——"

"Maybe I did and maybe I didn't," I said. "But you seemed to like it ! "

She said slowly : "Yes . . . I liked it. I suppose I'm one of those women who get a little bored sometimes and

47

look for adventure. But I'm *very* doubtful about you, Michael."

I said : " My dear girl, I, who am the soul of integrity. . . ."

She interrupted : " Yes ? Well, you may be the soul of integrity, but I'm beginning to suspect all sorts of things, Michael."

" Such as what ? " I asked.

She said : " Well, I lead a very normal ordinary quiet and restful life until I meet you on a golf course ; until you pretend to sprain your ankle. From that moment odd things happen which surprise me—but not *too* much. And then last night very late, or this morning very early, whichever you like to call it, something *quite* strange happens."

I said :

" Really ! This is most intriguing. I'm dying with curiosity. Tell me about it, Bettina."

She said slowly : " No, I don't think I will—not on the telephone. But if you'd *like* to come round to-night after dinner ; I'm having a little party here. It might amuse you and I *might* take you into a corner and tell you all about it."

I said : " I wonder is this really true ? Do you know I believe you've made up this very dramatic story just to get me along to your party. You can't resist me, can you, Bettina ? "

She laughed. She said softly : " You know, Michael, I told you last night you were a bit of a bastard and I was smiling when I said it. In a minute I shall tell you that you're a *lot* of one. Are you coming ? "

" Nothing can keep me away," I said. " I've got one or two things to do this evening, but with a bit of luck I shall be with you about half-past nine. I'd like that very much. Thank you very much indeed, Bettina. You're most kind to me."

" I don't know about that," she said. " Maybe I'll re-orientate my opinion of you. Maybe I shall want to know all sorts of things about you. I think you're very dangerous."

" Do you ? " I asked. " But then it strikes me that

you're the sort of woman who likes danger. It's amusing, isn't it ? It can be interesting."

She said doubtfully : " Yes, but not too much. Well, good-bye, Michael."

I said good-bye and hung up. I wondered what the hell had happened to Bettina.

At seven o'clock I changed my clothes, smoked a cigarette, drank a very small whisky and soda and went round to Verity Street. As I stood in front of the door waiting to put my finger on Janine's bellpush, an idea came into my head that this time the door wouldn't open ; that I should find that my bird had flown.

The idea was quite wrong. The door opened with its usual click, and I went up the stairs. Both the doors on Janine's landing were closed. I knocked on the door of the sitting-room ; stood waiting patiently, my hat in my hand. I realised, in the weird way that one does realise unimportant things, that waiting to see Janine gave me an odd thrill. I didn't know why. I couldn't understand it myself. As Bettina had so rightly pointed out I've told the tale to a hundred women in my lifetime, sometimes because it had been my job to do it, sometimes because I'd wanted to—you know what I mean. At the same time I couldn't quite understand the peculiar feeling of expectancy which I experienced whenever I came to Verity Street.

The door opened and Janine stood in the doorway holding the door wide open, with one arm outstretched resting on the door handle so that my entrance into the sitting-room was barred. It was obvious that she was just going out. I gave her a quick look ; realised that when Alison Fredericks had said she had some good clothes the girl was talking sense. Janine was superbly dressed.

She was wearing a black coat and skirt that had been cut by a *maestro*. Underneath was a duck-egg blue blouse in gorgette or some very soft silk, with tiny pleated frills at the neck. She wore a couple of diamond clips that had set somebody back for quite a piece of money, and her shoes and stockings were the last word. A small black tailor-made hat completed a picture.

She said in her low bored voice : " Oh, my God—so it's you again ! "

I gave her one of my most winsome smiles. I said : " Sorry if I'm annoying you. What are you going to do —talk to me or have me thrown out ? "

She sighed. She dropped her hand from the door-knob. She stood there, relaxed, bored, looking at me as if I was something the cat had brought in.

She asked : " Why do I have to talk to you ? What is there for us to talk about ? "

I said : " I want to talk about Sammy."

She said : " That's nonsense. I've told you all I know about him."

I shrugged my shoulders. I said politely : " Nuts ! "

She said : " My God ! You can be rude, can't you ? Very well, let's get it over. Will you come in, Mr.——" She waited for me to tell her my name. I didn't say anything. I went in.

She said : " I don't know your name. When I asked you last time you told me that it might be Santa Claus. You've got an odd idea of humour, haven't you ? "

I closed the door behind me, put my hat down on a chair. I said : " Listen, Janine. Don't make any mistakes about me. I can be very troublesome. On the other hand I'm quite a decent sort of cuss when you get to know me."

She took a cigarette from a box on the mantelpiece and lit it. She moved gracefully, slowly. I was intrigued to watch her.

She said : " The point is I don't particularly want to know you."

I said : " Maybe not, but you will. Like the poor I am always with you."

She lit the cigarette and looked at me through the flame of the lighter. She said : " Mr. Whoever-you-are, I'll take damned good care you're not always with me. I'm getting rather tired of you." She smiled slowly. " I'll tell you something else," she went on, " *I* can be tough too."

I nodded. " I can well believe that, Janine," I said.
" A woman who's as beautiful as you are, who's got what
you've got, who looks like you do, ought not to be kicking
around in a couple of furnished rooms in Verity Street—
not unless something's gone wrong somewhere. And when
things go wrong with beautiful ladies like you, they're
inclined to get tough. Sometimes they lash out blindly
in all directions, but only succeed in kicking themselves.
Be a good girl and take it easy."

She said, with the first hint of real anger I'd ever
heard in her voice. " I wonder why you think you can
be so damned insolent. I wonder why I don't have you
thrown out."

" I'll tell you," I said. " You're afraid. I'm the unknown, and at the present moment you're rather afraid
of the unknown."

She said : " Did you come here to discuss the unknown
with me ? Would you be very nice and tell me what it is
you want. I was just going out. I'm very busy. Shall
we make this interview as short as possible ? "

" Certainly," I said. I'd made up my mind on the
line I was going to take with Janine. I'd made up
my mind that I was going to take the line that the
white-faced rat had handed to me—simply because
there was a chance I might get some sort of reaction
from her.

I said : " Listen . . . Sammy Carew was a good
friend of mine. I know that the last place he visited
before his death was this apartment. You admitted that.
I want to find out one or two things about Sammy. I'm
not satisfied about him."

She said : " What do you mean by that ? "

" Listen to me, Janine," I said. " You told me that
Sammy left here early in the morning. All right. What
did he come here for ? "

She put her cigarette back into her mouth and inhaled.
She said : " What do you think ? "

I said : " Never mind what I think. I'm asking you a
question. You either want to answer it or you don't.
What did Sammy come here for ? "

She said : " What does a man like Carew go to a

woman's rooms in the small hours of the morning for ? What do you think, Mr. Clever Dick ? It's quite obvious that he came here to go to bed with me."

I said : " Well, that's a straight answer. Sammy always had a very good taste in women. But supposing I tell you that I don't believe that ? "

She said : " I don't know that I care very much what you believe. But will you tell me why you shouldn't believe it ? "

I said : " I came round here because I was told by that white-faced young gentleman who looked like a pansy that you and Sammy had left The Heap of Feathers not a very long time before I went there ; that he'd come back here with you. *You* told me that Sammy left early in the morning ; that he was killed by the flying-bomb in the Square near here."

She said : " It wasn't very difficult to check up on that, was it ? You went round to the mortuary in Elvaston Street and saw him."

I said : " I see . . . so you know where they took him. You went round and had a look yourself, did you ? You wanted to know that he was really dead. Or did you want to know something else ? "

She made a little moue of annoyance. She realised that she'd left her guard open for a moment ; that I'd slipped underneath it. She said :

" I didn't go round there. If I had, what should I want to find ? "

I said : " You might have wanted to find something that Sammy had on him when he was killed—something that you three people are rather interested in."

She looked at me. She said : " You're a most extraordinary man. Half the time I don't know what you're talking about. What three people ? "

I said : " Well, Janine, my small bouquet of flowers at the moment consists of three charming personalities— first a rather delightful woman of about forty with the most startling blue eyes, who for the sake of argument I will call Auntie—in fact she pretended to be Sammy's Aunt. The second flower in my little posy is the white-faced rat with the made-up mouth. The third person is yourself. Quite obviously, there's a very strong connection between the three of you, and I suppose you're going to tell me that you don't know anything about either of the other two ? "

She smiled wearily. She said : " I'm going to tell you just that thing. And how do you like that ? I don't know what you're talking about. I don't know any white-faced young man who makes up his mouth, and I don't know any blue-eyed ladies of forty."

" Sweet Janine, what a bloody little liar you are," I said.

Her eyes narrowed. She said : " I'm not used to being talked to like that."

" Maybe not," I said. " But I'm talking like it. Shall I tell you why I'm perfectly certain you know the lady of forty with the blue eyes ? Would you like to know ? "

She said casually : " I'm always enthralled by hearing you talk. One day I've no doubt if I listen long enough I'm going to hear something that really matters."

I said : " Well, I'll tell you something that matters now. Yesterday afternoon you expected a visit from Auntie, but you didn't want to meet her. So you went into your bedroom across the hallway and stood peering out of the window. You saw her coming down the street. When she was near the house you slipped out by the back way. You didn't mind her coming up here. You probably left the door open. You knew there was nothing in this room that would interest her except you. And that enables you to do what *you* wanted to do."

" How dramatic," she said. " How entirely thrilling and dramatic. And what did I do ? "

" You slipped round to Auntie's place at Kinnoul Street. Somehow—possibly you have a key—you got the door open. You went up to the room that Sammy had used. You looked round the place. You found his clothes on the bed. You found that somebody had cut out the linings of his coat and sewed them in rather badly. So you knew that somebody had been there first—somebody had got the thing that you were after. You were trying to find whatever it was that you and Auntie and the white-faced boy wanted. It was too bad there was nothing there.

"Then you went out. You went out in rather a hurry. I suppose you didn't want to meet Auntie on her way back. You went out in such a hurry you left the door unlatched. It was open when I went there later."

She said : "What a busybody you are. You seem to spend your whole life snooping about in other people's houses." Her face was suddenly illuminated by a charming smile. Her lovely lips parted and showed a flash of white teeth.

She said insolently : "Do tell me what it is you're looking for. I might be able to help you."

I said : "One of these days I'll tell you what I'm looking for. And in point of fact I'll have a bet with you that I'll find it."

She turned over her left wrist slowly and looked at a tiny gold wristwatch. She said : "I'm very sorry but this interview is at an end. I'm late now. I've no further information for you."

I looked at her for a moment. There was something very tough about this woman. In some novel that I had read some time—I'm a great reader of novels—I read something about a woman being like a steel blade. There was something about her that reminded me of the expression, although possibly the blade might not be of very good steel.

I shrugged my shoulders.

I said : "Well, it's been nice seeing you, Janine. I feel we shall meet again."

She said tautly : "You feel wrongly. I'd like to tell you something. Next time you come here I'm going to have you thrown out."

I smiled. "You'll have to get all your friends to help you," I said. "I'm a very tough person to throw out of a place where I want to stay put."

She said : "Yes. I think you are tough. But take some advice from me. Be a little more careful or your toughness won't help you a bit. And would you mind closing the door from the outside. I'm tired of you."

I picked up my hat. I said : "Good-bye, Janie."

I closed the door and I went down the stairs.

I arrived at Bettina's party at a quarter to ten. She lived on the first floor in an attractive block of mansion flats near Berkeley Square. The place was big, superbly furnished and had a definite air. Quite obviously Bettina was a person of taste and discernment.

Her drawing-room was long, high ceilinged, and with an " L " shaped piece and an alcove at the top. There was every sort of drink on the sideboard and the company looked as good as the furniture. There were four men and half a dozen women—well-bred types, and the woman —with one exception—good-looking if not beautiful. One—a Mrs. Heldon—would have taken first prize at a beauty competition. She intrigued me. She had a peculiar sort of tailor-made allure that looked as if it had been put on rather like a coat. I wondered what she was like when she wasn't being alluring. And I wondered just how long Bettina Vaile had known her.

The woman I liked the look of most of all was a Miss Varney—a tall, graceful girl with a fair skin and lovely hair to match. She wore a simple, very well-cut black frock with a string of pearls. The thought went through my head that she was the type that would have knocked Sammy for a row of pins. Standing by the sideboard, with a whisky and soda in my hand, murmuring sweet nothings to Mrs. Heldon, who smiled politely and said " yes " periodically—but who was obviously thinking about something else—I wondered just what Sammy would have thought of the set-up I had got myself into. I had a vague idea that he might have approved. He always believed in doing the thing that came into his head first and doing it in a very big way.

One of the men came up and joined in the conversation. I was glad to hear him begin to talk about himself. I thought Mrs. Heldon might as well say " yes " to him as to me. On the other side of the room, Bettina Vaile moved away from one of the other women and, as she did so, looked over her shoulder at me and gave a little familiar nod. I went over to her.

She said : " My room is at the end of the corridor on the right. Slip out and go there, Michael, when you get the chance. I want to talk to you."

She threw me a smile and went away.

I waited a few minutes ; then went out of the room. I walked down the long corridor into the room at the end. I closed the door behind me.

The room was a bedroom in white, with touches of blue and old gold. Everything about it was exquisite. There was a suggestion of perfume in the air. Altogether a very nice place. I sat down in the big chair in front of the high mirrored dressing-table. I wanted to light a cigarette but thought I'd better not.

The door opened and Bettina came in. She was wearing a red frock. She looked marvellous. As I got up she came over to me.

She said : " Well . . . Michael, aren't you going to kiss me ? Or are you afraid because this is my bedroom ? "

I grinned at her. I said : " I'll try anything once." I kissed her on the mouth. And liked it.

She sat down in the chair I had just vacated. She opened a drawer, took out cigarettes and gave me one.

" It's about time you did a little talking, Michael," she said. " I don't know what's at the back of your mind or what you're after. But I think you ought to let me in on it. Otherwise I might come to conclusions on my own without any assistance."

" What conclusions ? " I said.

She looked at the end of her cigarette. She said slowly, after a moment's hesitation : " I've an idea in my head that you're using me as a sort of stooge in some way or another. I don't know why I think that but the idea persists. I don't know anything about you, and I'm a little scared of you. I suppose this is because I think you look like a man ought to look and you talk and behave in a manner to match. You see, I'm quite honest with you. I'm rather *for* you and I think I ought to know quite a lot more about you, if only for my peace of mind. Well . . . ? "

I stood looking down at her. I thought : To hell with this. Now you've started something, and it's going the wrong way. Why in the name of everything that's holy must this sort of thing happen ?

I said : " Well . . . there isn't a great deal to know about me. I'm quite an obvious sort of person."

She shook her head. " You're nothing of the sort, my sweet," she said. " You're a damned dangerous man—I knew that from the start. In fact, I think you're a spy or something. I believe you've pulled a very fast one on me that I don't know anything about. Right ? "

" Nonsense, Bettina," I said : " You've been reading thrillers. But where are you getting all these funny ideas from ? " I picked up my whisky and soda from the mantelpiece where I had put it. As I drank it I could see her looking at me sideways with a small and quite charming smile curving her mouth.

She was looked at herself in the dressing-table mirror and arranged a straying curl. Then she knocked the ash from her cigarette. I had the idea that she was trying to arrange her ideas ; that she was going to be a trifle difficult—or was she ?

She said softly : " Ever since I've known you, Michael, the oddest things have happened. Last night I had the strangest idea that I was being followed. The idea persisted until I *really* began to believe it. Then, when I got back here eventually, I persuaded myself that I was being foolish ; that I was using my imagination a trifle too much. Well . . . I went to bed and when I'd been in bed for ten minutes or so somebody tried to shoot me through the window."

She turned round on the chair and looked at me. She was still smiling but her eyes were worried.

I said : " What the hell do you mean, Bettina ? Do you really mean to tell me that someone tried to shoot you through your own bedroom window ? I can't believe it. It's not possible."

" Go and look at the window," she said. " And then come here and I'll show you the bullet. It actually cut a groove across the coverlet and went into the wall on the other side of the room. You can see the mark. I dug it out with some nail scissors."

I walked round the big double bed and examined the

window. It was a bullet hole all right. Fired from fairly close range. I opened the window and looked out. Outside there was a courtyard with a fountain in the centre. Opposite some fifty yards away were the flats on the other side of the fountain.

I asked : " Who lives in those flats opposite ? The one immediately opposite your window, the one above that and the one below that ? " It was obvious to me that the bullet had been fired from one of those flats.

Bettina said : " Nobody does. They're empty. Michael come here and look at the bullet."

I took it from her. I've seen that sort of splayed bronze coloured slug before. The sort of thing that's fired from a .40 Schmeisser rifle to which somebody had obviously taken the trouble to fit a silencer.

She said : " Well . . . what's to do about it, Michael ? "

I lit a fresh cigarette and took a long time about the process. Candidly, I didn't like the way things were going. Bettina was nobody's fool. She was suspicious. She might easily start something.

I shrugged my shoulders.

She said : " You see, Michael, it's quite obvious to me that someone thinks I· have something to do with you . . . somebody who doesn't like you—or your friends— very much. And *I* don't know what to think." She laughed softly. " After all, that business about your ankle was very suspicious, wasn't it ? "

I thought I might as well bring things to a head. I said : " It seems to me that the best thing you can do is to go to the Police. After all you can't have people shooting at you in bed. It's a most uncomfortable business."

She nodded. " Quite," she said in the same soft and delightfully caressing voice. " But if I go to the police they might ask me all sorts of inconvenient questions, mightn't they, Michael ? They might want to check up on the people immediately around me. They might ask me questions about you—questions that I couldn't possibly answer." She smiled at me. Her eyes were bright and mischievous.

I didn't say anything. I was busily engaged in mentally

kicking myself. It looked as if—far from my making a stooge out of Bettina, she was, at the moment, taking a delight in reversing the process.

She said : " I know one or two people in the police —high up people I mean—and I've no doubt that they'd help if anything like this happened again. You see, it *is* rather frightening, Michael, isn't it ? But I'm certain in my mind that this business has something to do with you. I'm *certain* of it. Darling, the least you can do is to be straight with me. Or aren't you ever straight with anyone ? "

I said : " Move up." I sat down on the chair beside her and took her hand. She laid her face against mine.

She murmured : " Tell me the truth, Michael. I'm *for* you. I'll play if you'll let me. But I'm certain you've been up to something, that you're in some sort of a jam and that you've been using me as a stooge. Well . . . I don't mind. Not so long as I know what it's all about. But I've *got* to know."

I thought there was only one thing to do about it. At the moment I certainly could not afford to take a chance on Bettina starting something ; going to the police and generally putting the tin lid on everything. I thought that the Old Man would be goddamned pleased if he knew the way things were shaping. *Any* sort of publicity and he would tear me wide open.

I said : " Listen, Bettina. Maybe there's something in your guess, but I don't want to talk about it to-night. I'll have a very straight talk to you to-morrow and we'll certainly have to do something about the boyo who's taking pot shots at you through windows."

" I'll do just what you like, my dear," she said. " But quite obviously, *something* must be done. . . ."

I thought : You're telling me . . . !

I said : " Listen, Bettina, there's a young woman I know. She's rather a brainy type and quite resourceful. She's also very tough. I think I'll get in touch with her to-night and ask her to come round here. I think she'd better stay with you for a few days until we see how things are going."

" I knew I was right about you," she said. " I'm sure

story wasn't true ; even if your own version was correct, and Sammy left your place fairly early in the morning ; you'd still be the last person that he was seen alive with."

She said : " You're presupposing of course that he left my apartment and went straight round to the Square. You're presupposing that he didn't go anywhere else first."

I said : " I'm not presupposing anything. I'm only interested in facts, and eventually, believe it or not, Janine, some fact is going to emerge—something that I can get my teeth into."

She made a little clicking noise with her tongue. She said : " *Then* it's going to be fearfully interesting, isn't it ? I should love to see you snap into action—isn't that what they call it ? "

I didn't say anything. We were halfway down St. James's Street. I turned off and rang the bell at Sasha's. I wondered if she'd be there. In the old days she used to have a party every night.

She was there. After a few minutes the door opened and she stood in the dimly light hallway. She said :

" Well . . . well . . . ! If it isn't Michael. Where have you come from ? How nice to see you again."

I said : " It's nice to see you, Sasha. This is a remote cousin of mine—Miss Janine. Do you think we might have a drink ? "

" Of course," said Sasha. " That's what we're here for."

We went up the stairs into the long sitting-room. The place wasn't too crowded—just the usual conglomeration of Services, and a few pretty ladies.

I said a few words to Sasha, and then piloted Janine over to a table at the end of the room. I went over to the serving sideboard and got a couple of whiskies and sodas. I went back to her. I said :

" Well, mysterious lady, here's the drink. And here's a cigarette. And where do we go from there ? "

I lit her cigarette for her, While I was doing it I looked at her closely. It's a funny thing but I've noticed that all the really bad women I've met in my life are rather beautiful and if they're not exactly beautiful they've got a gerous," she murmured, " which is the reason I go for you, I suppose. Good-night, my sweet."

I finished my drink, got my hat from the hallway, went down the stairs.

I was in a hell of a temper. It seemed as if my scheme with Bettina had been *too* successful. Unless I was very careful she could make things damned inconvenient. Something would have to be done about Bettina.

The big cool entrance hall on the ground floor was dark. As I neared the swing doors a small voice from a dark corner behind a large palm said : " Mr. Kells. . . ."

It was Alison Fredericks. I stopped, took out my cigarette case and made a big business of lighting a cigarette. I said under my breath, looking straight in front of me :

" Well . . . what is it ? "

" Janine's on your tail," she said. " She's on the other side of the courtyard in one of the doorways waiting for you to come out. She's quite clever, that one. It isn't the first time she's done that sort of thing."

" Thanks for the tip," I said. " Now listen. Go up to No. 15 on the first floor—Mrs. Bettina Vaile. Introduce yourself. She knows about you. Stick by her and keep your eyes skinned. Somebody tried to knock her off last night. I'll telephone you to-morrow. But for the love of mike look after her."

" Very well, Mr. Kells," she said.

I went through the swing doors. I stood outside so that Janine could take a really good look and know it was me.

I thought the time was coming when I should have to do something about this Janine. She was beginning to get in my hair.

But everything was beginning to get in my hair. I've handled one or two jobs in my time that weren't easy ones, but this business was beginning to get on my nerves. Things just happened and no one knew why. I knew just about as much as when I started on the job.

I wondered why the hell Sammy had had to get cockeyed on the night of that party. That was the night he was supposed to talk to me. But he'd ducked talking to me. He'd evaded me—which wasn't a bit like Sammy. Why?

I stood there in front of the swing doors thinking about the party. I'd been a little cut myself of course. In fact half an hour after I'd got there I was definitely cut. It had seemed indicated. Sammy wasn't going to do any business and was obviously giving himself a night off.

I began to remember flashes from that party. I remembered a face here and there. I remembered the woman —the attractive one who'd worn a cornflower blue frock . . .

That woman had been Janine! Now I remembered. It had been Janine. And that was probably the reason why Sammy wouldn't talk. He knew she was there and he knew why she was there. The fact that she *was* there had made him keep away from me.

Because, knowing he'd had one or two, he was afraid to say or do anything in case he gave something away.

So that was it!

And now, waiting on the other side of the fountain was Janine. Waiting for *me*. I wondered just how much she'd had to do with Sammy's death. Just what had happened on that day after the party.

I thought: All right, baby . . . you play it along your way for the moment. But before I'm through, you'll wonder what's hit you!

CHAPTER FOUR

ALISON

I WALKED slowly out of the courtyard past the fountain, through the arch that led into the main street. I walked very slowly, drawing on my cigarette, looking nonchalant. I had no doubt that somewhere behind me in the shadows Janine was following. She was no fool, and somebody had taught her to put rubber tips on her high heels. I could hear nothing behind me in the deserted street.

I wondered what the hell she was playing at : what her

idea was. Incidentally, I supposed she was thinking the same thing about me. We all seemed to be chasing each other round in circles—nobody knowing anything very much—everyone trying fast ones when they could. I wondered what the Old Man would have thought of it. At the moment I didn't propose to give him an opportunity of thinking anything. His language, faced with the present situation, would have been a trifle too caustic for my liking. I thought I'd wait till something tangible happened. If it ever did happen.

I turned into Charles Street and began to walk in the direction of Berkeley Square. I crossed the Square ; went into the telephone box at the bottom of Hay Hill. I called through to Freeby. I heard the ringing note ; wondered if he'd be in. I was relieved when I heard his voice.

I said : " Listen, Freeby, this is Kells. You can lay off Mrs. Vaile. I've put somebody else on to her."

He said : " All right. Is there anything else ? "

I said : " Yes. At the present moment I've got a very charming lady called Janine, who lives at 16 Verity Street, S.W., on my tail. She seems to have ideas about me. I propose that you transfer your attentions from Mrs. Vaile to her. In the meantime you might go round to 16 Verity Street ; see if you can get in without raising the whole neighbourhood. Take a look round her apartment. She's got two rooms—a bedroom and a sitting-room—on the first floor landing. There's a back door, which I should think would be the easiest way to get in, and a landlady on the ground floor. If you think it's too dangerous to try it without raising the whole neighbourhood, lay off till you get an opportunity. We've got enough trouble as it is."

He said : " All right. I understand. I take it things aren't going so well."

" Things aren't going at all," I said. " Good-night. Get in touch with me if anything happens. I'll probably ring you soon."

He said good-night and hung up.

I came out of the telephone box, walked quickly up Hay Hill, turned into Dover Street. When I got round the corner I shot into a doorway. I stood there, inhaling cigarette smoke, waiting for Janine. After a minute or so she went past. She was walking quickly, very quietly and with delightful grace. She had rubber tips on her heels all right, and she knew how to do the job. I let her walk a few yards past my doorway ; then I came out. I went after her. I said :

"Good-evening, Janine. How are you ? Is this your usual beat, or were you by any chance looking for me ? "

She stopped, turned round. She was a pretty cool customer, was Janine. She didn't turn a hair.

She said : "Oh ! So it's you." There was just the right inflection of surprise in her voice.

I said : "Yes, it's me. You're amazed to see me, aren't you ? You haven't been on my tail the whole evening ? What is it you want, sweet ? "

She said : "I don't think I want anything particularly except a drink. I think I'd like to smoke a cigarette and have a drink."

I thought to myself : You've got your nerve, my girl. I wondered what the new idea was.

I said : "Well, that should be easily arranged. Come with me. I think I know where we can get a drink even if it is a little after hours. It's a lovely evening, isn't it ? "

She said : "I suppose it is."

We began to walk down Dover Street. Nobody said anything. After quite a while she said in a soft and rather hesitant sort of voice :

"You know, eventually someone has to do a little talking. I wonder which of us it's going to be."

I said : "I'll tell you, Janine. It's going to be you. I don't have to talk unless I want to, but you'll *have* to in a minute."

She said : "Yes ? Why ? "

I said : "I'll tell you why. You had *something* to do with Sammy. I might as well tell you now that Sammy wasn't killed by any flying-bomb. He was murdered. I think someone shot him."

The news didn't seem to perturb her a great deal. She said : "Oh ? Well, that rather cuts out your little story about my being the last person who was with him, doesn't it ? "

I said : "Not at all. Even if the white-faced boyo's

story wasn't true ; even if your own version was correct, and Sammy left your place fairly early in the morning ; you'd still be the last person that he was seen alive with."

She said : " You're presupposing of course that he left my apartment and went straight round to the Square. You're presupposing that he didn't go anywhere else first."

I said : " I'm not presupposing anything. I'm only interested in facts, and eventually, believe it or not, Janine, some fact is going to emerge—something that I can get my teeth into."

She made a little clicking noise with her tongue. She said : " *Then* it's going to be fearfully interesting, isn't it ? I should love to see you snap into action—isn't that what they call it ? "

I didn't say anything. We were halfway down St. James's Street. I turned off and rang the bell at Sasha's. I wondered if she'd be there. In the old days she used to have a party every night.

She was there. After a few minutes the door opened and she stood in the dimly light hallway. She said :

" Well . . . well . . . ! If it isn't Michael. Where have you come from ? How nice to see you again."

I said : " It's nice to see you, Sasha. This is a remote cousin of mine—Miss Janine. Do you think we might have a drink ? "

" Of course," said Sasha. " That's what we're here for."

We went up the stairs into the long sitting-room. The place wasn't too crowded—just the usual conglomeration of Services, and a few pretty ladies.

I said a few words to Sasha, and then piloted Janine over to a table at the end of the room. I went over to the serving sideboard and got a couple of whiskies and sodas. I went back to her. I said :

" Well, mysterious lady, here's the drink. And here's a cigarette. And where do we go from there ? "

I lit her cigarette for her. While I was doing it I looked at her closely. It's a funny thing but I've noticed that all the really bad women I've met in my life are rather beautiful and if they're not exactly beautiful they've got a strange sort of attraction (which I suppose is the reason why they're bad). Janine had it. Everything about her was quite delightful. The duck-egg chiffon blouse she wore beneath her black coat, with its tiny ruffles at the throat, was perfect, meticulously spotless. Her teeth were like little pearls, her hands exquisitely manicured. I've met a lot of women in my life of all sorts, shapes, sizes and conditions. Some of them have intrigued me and some have bored me, but I was very intrigued with Janine.

I said : " Well, now what ? "

There was a little silence. She drew on her cigarette. I noticed that her fingers were trembling a little.

She said : " Of course you think that I've been following you this evening, don't you ? "

I said : " I don't think it. I know it. Haven't you ? "

She hesitated ; then : " Yes, I suppose I have. But not because I wanted to watch what you were doing. Believe it or not, I wanted to talk to you. When I saw you go into the place near Berkeley Square I thought I'd wait till you came out ; then I'd come up to you and speak to you."

I said : " Well, why didn't you ? "

She said coolly : " You went away too quickly. I hadn't a chance."

I said : " Janine, you're very beautiful but you're not at all an accomplished liar. You had heaps of opportunities to speak to me before I got out of the courtyard. Anyway, let's cut out the frills. What's it all about ? But I ought to warn you."

She sighed. " Dear . . . dear . . . you're always warning me, aren't you ? "

I said : " Well, I don't know about that, but I'm warning you *now*. You know, I'm getting a little bit impatient. So far as you're concerned I've been running round in circles. I'm rather bored with the process. I think it's time that you and I got down to hard tacks."

She said : " That's exactly what I propose to do. But before we do it, can I ask you a question ? "

I began to laugh inside. Quite obviously, she was doing exactly the same thing as I was—bluffing, trying to find out as much as she could without giving anything away.

I thought this might be a very interesting conversation.

I said : " Providing there's only *one* question I might answer it, when I know what it is."

She said : " I can quite understand your being interested in Sammy Carew's death. He was your friend. But you know that he *is* dead. So I don't see now what you're worrying about unless there's something else—unless you're interested in something else beyond knowing that Mr. Carew is actually dead."

I said : " Possibly I am. Why shouldn't I be ? "

She nodded. She said : " Why don't you tell me what it is you're really interested in."

I thought I'd try a shot in the dark—another fast one. I said : " Believe it or not I'm interested in exactly the same thing as you, Auntie and the white-faced rat, are interested in. Now we know where we are, don't we ? "

She shook her head. She said : " No, we don't know where we are. I don't even know what you're talking about. You couldn't possibly be interested in the thing that I want."

I said : " All right, I couldn't be. But I'm sick of talking in riddles. What is it ? "

She raised her eyebrows. She said : " Don't you think a woman is entitled to be interested in her own marriage certificate ? "

I nearly fell off my chair. I looked at her for a moment. I said : " So you're interested in a marriage certificate. I suppose Sammy had your marriage lines on him when he was killed, and you want them."

She said : " That's perfectly right. He had them and I want them."

I said : " All right. I'll believe anything once just for a few minutes. Now tell me something else—why should Sammy have your marriage lines ? "

Her eyes opened wide. I believe I've said before that she had rather lovely eyes—guileless, translucent eyes. She looked at me for quite a few seconds.

" But of course Sammy ought to have them. You see he was my husband."

I didn't say anything. I picked up my whisky and soda and took a long drink. Then I looked at her with almost admiration in my heart. Then a little doubt crept into my mind. You never knew with Sammy. I hesitated about that one. Surely Sammy wouldn't do a thing like that ; surely Sammy wouldn't get himself married to some woman he didn't know anything much about—not at a time like this—not with what he had on his plate—unless . . .

The idea wasn't impossible, of course. Sammy was so keen, so enthusiastic, that he'd do anything, if he felt it was indicated. Supposing he had married this woman temporarily, because he had some sort of ulterior motive. But I still couldn't understand it.

I grinned at her. " So you're Mrs. Carew ? Well . . . well . . . well . . . I don't believe you."

She said : " I'm not worrying about that. You asked me what I wanted from Sammy and I've told you. You knew that I'd been round to the mortuary at Elvaston Street. Well, the police told me who he was. They showed me the things they found on him but the marriage certificate was gone."

I began to see daylight. I said : " I see. So the only proof that you were Sammy's wife and entitled to such things as you wanted that were found in his possession when he was killed, was missing. But it was a very good try-on, wasn't it—a very sound idea ? "

I took another drink. " It shouldn't worry you, Janine," I said. " After all if you were married there'll be an entry in a registry somewhere. There was a registrar or a clergyman. There were witnesses. Even if this very valuable document is missing, you can easily prove that you were married to Sammy, if you were married."

She said : " I'm afraid not. It's not quite so easy. You see, we weren't married in this country." She looked at me. She smiled.

I gave up. I realised for once in my life I was up against something that was very tough, very clever—just as tough, just as clever, as I was. Maybe more clever than I was.

I said : " You're not drinking your whisky."

She picked up the glass, drank a little. She looked at me over the rim. She said :

" I must go in a minute. It's been very nice meeting you."

I said : " That's kind of you, Janine."

She said slowly : " No. I like your type. You're rather forthright. You can be very rude. You know that you're quite an attractive man. You know you're quite clever. You know you're awfully tough. I'm rather suspicious of you and I don't think I trust you a great deal, but I think it would be a very good idea, for your sake anyway, if we were friends."

I said : " That sounds remarkably like a threat."

She said : " You take it any way you like, but be very nice and don't bother me any more. If you do I'm going to be angry with you."

I put on a very serious expression. I said : " And then what ? "

She said : " You'll see." She got up. She said : " Don't bother to come downstairs. I'm certain I shall be able to get a cab. Have another drink and relax. Good-night."

She walked across the room, smiled at Sasha, who was serving drinks at the sideboard, went through the door at the other end. I took my empty glass over to have it re-filled. I thought to myself : Well, I'll be damned !

I went back to my table, sat down, lit a fresh cigarette and thought about Janine. I knew *one* thing about her. She had one hell of a nerve and she'd stop at nothing. Her attitude had been deliberately challenging and, as she wasn't a woman who'd take an unnecessary chance just for the fun of doing so, she had something up her sleeve. She knew, somehow, that I'd got to play this job care-fully ; that I couldn't frame her, or have her removed quietly. Only if she thought along those lines could she afford to be so damned sure of herself.

Well . . . why couldn't she be framed ? I'd framed women as clever as Janine in my time when the process had been necessary.

A vague suggestion of the perfume she had been wear-ing seemed to hang about the table. She was a hell of a woman. A woman with that peculiar quality of allure that is independent of looks. And she had those too.

And she was sure of herself. Somehow the idea persisted that she thought she held the trump card. I wondered what it could be.

I wondered if *she* had the thing that everyone—Auntie, the white-faced rat and Heaven knows who else—wanted.

Maybe *she* had it. Maybe she was giving all of us the run-around.

I shrugged my shoulders and finished my whisky.

I walked home. Piccadilly was deserted. It was a lovely night with a moon. Walking down the wide street I turned over in my mind the rather extraordinary series of circumstances which had happened since I'd started on this business.

I took myself to task. I wondered exactly what I should say to the Old Man if he were to telephone through to me and ask me what the position was. All I could tell him was that since my last interview with him I had talked to Janine, picked up Bettina Vaile on a golf course, had a few drinks at her party, heard that somebody had tried to shoot her through a window. Not a satisfactory report I thought.

But now in any event I realised one fact. Janine was the woman who had been at the cocktail party on the night before Sammy's death. Now I remembered her definitely. She had been the woman who was there. This gave me ideas. Here was probably the explanation for Sammy's not wanting to talk to me—because she was there. And this fact stamped her as somebody who was very dangerous—somebody to be watched very carefully.

When I arrived at my apartment I found a note from the hall porter waiting for me. The note was terse. It said : " *A gentleman would like Mr. Kells to telephone him. Grosvenor* 77650." I threw my hat into a corner and went to the telephone. I wondered who the gentleman was. Possibly it was Freeby.

I was wrong. It was the Old Man. And he sounded like Hell. He said :

" Hello, Kells. I'm at 71 Great Grosvenor Court. If

you're not doing anything *very* important you might like to come round. I'd like to talk to you."

I said I'd go round right away. I didn't like the sound of the Old Man. He sounded as if " he'd had it." And that meant that somebody else was going to have it too. I'd an idea that that somebody was going to be me.

The place was a rather good flat just off Grosvenor Crescent. I supposed it was just *one* of the Old Man's hangouts. He had dozens of them. It was very well-furnished, very comfortable. He was sitting in a big chair with a small table at his elbow with cigars and whisky and cigarettes. He was wearing a plum-coloured velvet dressing-gown, and he looked like the wrath of God !

He said : " Put your hat down and give yourself a whisky and soda and a cigarette. Then sit down and listen."

I did all that.

He sat very still and looked at me. Then he put his cigar in his mouth and smoked for a bit. Then he took it out of his mouth and looked at me some more.

I knew what it was all about. Nothing had happened, and the Old Man liked things to happen. He hadn't heard a word from me and he deduced that I was lying down on the job. Everyone knew the Old Man's technique. He picked a man for a job and had a bet with himself that he'd picked the right man. Usually he did. He then sat back and waited for results. *And there had to be results*. Otherwise the Old Man could get very annoyed.

He was very old-fashioned about getting results and it seemed that he was going to be slightly old-fashioned with me.

Eventually he said : " You're supposed to be a damned good agent. You're supposed to be one of the three best men in the business. That means that you're supposed to have a damned good nerve and brains and initiative. I said *supposed*. The operative word is *supposed*. You understand ? "

I didn't say anything. I was fed up. I thought : All right . . . if you want to be goddamned rude, *be* rude. It's not doing you any good and it's not doing me any harm.

71

He was right about me being a good agent. As for being *one* of the best three that was hooey. I was *the* best and he knew it—especially now that Sammy was out of business. And I felt a little annoyed with him. I've taken more goddamned chances for the Old Man in half a dozen countries than any of the others of his hand-picked menagerie. And he knew it. And he knew *I* knew it. I thought to hell with it !

And the whisky was *very* good. It was pre-war twenty under proof whisky. I gave myself another shot of it.

He went on : " You and Sammy Carew were *supposed* to be a damned good team. Well, have a look ! It's not very good, is it ? Carew seems to have got himself knocked out of the game before he even had a chance to talk to you. But you connected with him. You two were together and you didn't do anything about it. You didn't do anything about it because both of you got damned drunk at that party—the party that happened the night before he was killed. Well ? "

I went on smoking. I didn't say anything. There wasn't, just at that moment, anything to say.

He said : " All right. Well . . . that was that. You were handed the buck. And what have you done ? " He made a funny noise halfway between an expression of disgust and a curse. He repeated : " What have you done ? Sweet nothing . . . sweet Fanny Adams ! And look what I get. Look at the sort of stuff *I* have to put up with because I use nitwits like you."

He slung a " Very Secret " letter across to me. It was from a very high-up one. It reminded the Old Man, very politely, very diplomatically, that the flying-bomb casualties in Southern England were becoming a little more heavy than heretofore. It suggested, having regard to th places where the last few lots had descended, during the last three or four nights, that possibly the Germans had some idea as to where they were shooting the goddamned things. It pointed out a lot of things. In a polite way it was extremely tough.

I sighed. I handed it back to the Old Man.

I said casually : " So what ? "

That tore it. The Old Man went red in the face and

told me all about myself. He called me everything he could lay his tongue to. He was very unpleasant. I didn't say anything because nobody ever does say anything when the Old Man loses his temper. Incidentally, I'm very fond of him, and I knew that most of it was bull. He's like that.

When he finished I said : " Listen to me for a moment, sir. I think you're rather making a mistake about this party of ours. The one we got drunk at. Remember, if you please, that Sammy and I hadn't met for some time. The last time we connected we were a couple of German Junior Artillery Officers playing around on the rocket stations in the Pas de Calais. When Carew was put on this assignment over here he played it his own way. I didn't know anything about the job, or what he was doing or why. Neither did you. Possibly *he* didn't know a great deal either. But when I went to that party and saw that Sammy was cockeyed I knew it was good enough for me to get cockeyed. So I got cockeyed. And that was that."

He asked : " Why was it good enough ? "

I said : " There was a woman there. A lovely piece of work called Janine. She's working on the other side. I think Sammy was wise to her. He knew damned well that she was waiting to see *who* he was going to contact. That's why he wouldn't talk to me. He was trying to keep her from getting wise to me. That's why he got cut. He knew that if she saw him getting cut she'd think he wasn't working. Because an operative like Sammy doesn't get high when he's working. I got drunk for the same reason. And its no good *pretending* to be drunk. You have to get *drunk*—then they *believe* it. I got his address and that was all, and after that he steered away from me as if I'd got the plague. Because he was scared of that woman."

I paused for some breath and a little whisky.

" None of this was any good," I said. " No damned good to anybody, because they got Sammy next day. But I know the woman. I know the woman who was at that party."

The Old Man grunted. He said : " Well, that's something. You'd better do something about her, or to her, or something. I don't want to get letters like that one. I don't want to. I'm not used to it. For God's sake, Michael get cracking. I know these flying-bombs aren't a good military weapon. But they're not a health treatment either. And maybe there's something worse coming. All right . . . have another drink and get going."

I got up. I poured another drink and drank it at a gulp.

I walked over to the door. I looked back at him and grinned. I said : " Good-night, sir."

He twisted his face at me. Then he began to smile. He said : " Good-night, and damn your eyes, and remember what I told you."

I closed the door quietly behind me.

I walked round the streets for a considerable time. Then I went home. I took a hot bath, gave myself a large whisky and soda, went to bed. I came to the conclusion that sleep was really the only thing that was interesting. I switched off the light and lay for some time, my hands clapsed behind my head trying to pick up some definite point in all this conglomeration of theories—something that I could get my fingers on—something that would give me a pointer. I lay there for a considerable time wondering about Sammy, and Auntie, Janine, the white-faced rat ; this quartet, which at the moment, formed the basis of my not too successful investigation.

I gave it up. As I have said before, it has always seemed to me that in a job like this the only thing to do is to follow one's nose. I decided to go to sleep, and with this decision the telephone jangled. I sighed heavily and took up the receiver. It was Bettina.

She said : " I hope I haven't disturbed you, Michael, have I ? "

I said : " Not exactly. I'm in bed. I was just going to sleep. I've been thinking."

She said : " I'm afraid I'm going to give you something else to think about."

I said : " That doesn't surprise me. What's worrying you, Bettina ? "

She said slowly : " Well, I'm worried about this Alison Fredericks of yours. She's a nice girl, isn't she ? I like her a great deal."

I said : " Why should you worry about her ? " My voice was a little bad-tempered.

She said : " Dear, you wouldn't be angry, would you. I'm doing my best to help even although at the moment I don't know anything about you, even if I am poised almost on my toes to hear what you're going to tell me to-morrow. I'm still trying to do my best for you."

I said : " That's very sweet of you, Bettina."

She said : " You're terrible, aren't you, Michael ? You just won't let any woman be fond of you. You're like a hedgehog all the time. You put your prickles out."

I said : " All right, I'm like a hedgehog. And where do we go from there ? Tell my why you're worried about Alison Fredericks ? "

She said : " I'll tell you. Not very long after you left she came to the flat. She introduced herself to me. By this time the party was over. Everybody had gone—that is everybody except Mrs. Heldon. Alison and Mrs. Heldon and I had a drink together and then Mrs. Heldon left. Alison and I let our hair down and had a heart-to-heart talk. I'm afraid most of the talking was done by me."

I laughed into the telephone. I said : " I bet you tried to pump her about me good *and* plenty. Didn't you, honey-lamb ? "

She gurgled. " You bet I did," she said. " And what would you have done? When a woman who is as nice as I am, as rich as I am, and as stupid as I *can* be, falls for a tough, good-looking, scoundrel like you, she's entitled to try and look after herself—a little anyway. If she *can*— which I very much doubt."

I said : " All right. So you tried to pump Alison Fredericks, and she told you sweet nothing at all. Right ? "

" Right," said Bettina. " She just steered the conversation away from you. She's a clever little thing, isn't she ? However, it was obvious that she knew about the attempt that had been made to shoot me. She told me about that, so it was obvious that you'd told her about it. All right. We decided that I wouldn't sleep in my room ; that we'd go into another room in which there are two small beds. We had some tea and we went to bed. Are you still interested ? "

I said : " I'm very interested. These domestic details thrill me."

She said : " Well, I hope they're going to remain domestic. But the thing is that about twenty minutes after we'd gone to bed the telephone bell rang. I suppose I was a little bit nervous. I wondered who it might be. Alison said that she would answer the telephone. She answered it. She listened for a little while ; then she said : ' Very well, I understand.' It was you of course who was speaking to her."

I said : " What the hell do you mean, Bettina ? *I* wasn't speaking to her. I haven't telephoned your flat to-night."

She said : " Oh dear . . . "

I said : " Listen, what did she say to you ? "

She said : " She came back to the bedroom and said that she'd had a message from you ; that she was to go to a place to meet you ; that it was very urgent."

I said : " What place ? "

She answered quickly : " I've got the address. I was clever about that. I made her write it down—a place called 27 Namur Street. She was to go there to meet you."

I said : " I see . . . so she was to go to 27 Namur Street and meet me ? What did she do ? "

She said : " Well, she got up and she went."

I heaved a sigh. I didn't like the sound of this at all. I said : " Then what ? "

She said : " Nothing after that. I went to bed, but I couldn't sleep. I thought it a little bit odd that you should come through here and speak to her and not say anything to me." I heard her laugh softly. " I thought at least you might have said a few words to me. Then when she didn't come back I got really worried. I've lain here in the darkness for such a long time worrying about her, and incidentally worrying a little about you."

I laughed. I said : " But why worry about me ? "

She said : " Of course you wouldn't know, would you ? You wouldn't know that I'm rather fond of you, Michael ? You wouldn't know that I think you're rather an odd person ; that somehow I've an idea in my head that you're

playing with fire. Anyway, I've been lying here. I've
been very unhappy. Eventually, I made up my mind
that I'd come through to you and talk to you. So it
wasn't you who telephoned Alison ? "

I thought quickly. Quite candidly, I didn't think it
was going to be a good thing to let Bettina into every
phase of this game. She was beginning to know a little
too much, and what would one more lie matter ?

I said : " Well, candidly, Bettina, to tell you the truth
I *did* telephone through. I did ask Alison to meet me. I
wanted to talk to her."

She said : " So you've seen her ? "

I said : " No, I've been rather busy, but I shall. In
the meantime you go back to bed—relax. You can take
it from me that nothing is going to happen to-night.
Nothing exciting, I mean. I'll come round about twelve
to-morrow and drink a cocktail with you. Then we'll
lunch together. Would you like that ? "

She said : " Of course, Michael. I'd like it very much."

I said : " All right. So long, Bettina."

There was a little pause ; then she said in rather a
husky voice with a suggestion of tears in it : " Good-
night, my darling."

I hung up.

I went into the bathroom and drank a glass of water. I
wondered what the hell was breaking now. I wondered
who it was had telephoned Alison ; had given such a
good imitation of my voice—or had said they were
talking for me. Immediately to my mind there came the
picture of Janine—the soft-footed lady who had been on
my tail most of the evening, who had known that I'd
gone to see Bettina, who'd probably known that Alison
had gone there too. I thought maybe I'd been a fool about
Janine. I thought that possibly if I'd had any sense, if I
hadn't thought quite so much of myself, I should have
done something about Janine some time ago and not let
her run about spare making any mischief she wanted to
make. I knew goddam well that if I'd rung the Old Man
and asked him to fix her he'd have fixed her somehow.
But I hadn't rung the Old Man. I hadn't rung him because . . . well, it was part of the tradition in our rather

odd business that we tried to play it the best way we could ourselves without dragging other people into the job. But I wasn't quite certain that I'd been justified in my attitude.

I went back to the sitting-room, lit a cigarette, drank a small whisky and soda. I tried to make some sort of sense out of all this business. In any event I didn't see who could do any good by getting into touch with Alison. I could understand somebody wanting to get at *me*.

I started to put on some clothes. I wasn't too pleased with life. I'd made up my mind to a plan of action. I thought that with Alison Fredericks looking after Bettina, and the enterprising Freeby keeping an eye on Janine ; with myself playing around supervising everything, within a few days I should have put my finger on some salient fact—something from which I could have worked. But it seemed to me that most of the things I'd done had repercussed on me rather badly.

Bettina, for instance. I'd played her for a stooge, but she wasn't very much of a stooge. She'd got wise to me fairly quickly. Janine had been very much more clever than I thought she was going to be and I wondered what the hell Auntie was doing. She'd probably show up and start something in a minute. It was with a sense of relief that I realised that I'd knocked off the white-faced rat. If I hadn't he'd probably be starting something too.

I finished dressing, looked round the flat, put on my hat and went out. When I was in the corridor outside the front door I got one of those funny ideas. I went back and got the Mauser automatic and stuck it in the pocket under my left arm. It gave me a sense of comfort. I wondered where the hell Namur Street was. I went out into the street.

I walked along in the direction of Knightsbridge. At the intersection of Knightsbridge and Wilton Place, I met a War Reserve policeman. I asked him where Namur Street was. He told me it was a turning off Mulbery Street, about twelve minutes away. I thanked him and began to walk slowly in the direction of Mulbery Street.

I thought this was a little bit odd. This business had

started off at Mulbery Street. The job had really started in the Heap of Feathers. I thought it was an extraordinary coincidence that this Namur Street should be off Mulbery Street. But was it a coincidence? There was Janine living in Verity Street just around the corner. There was the Heap of Feathers where I'd met White-Face in Mulbery Street. After all, there was nothing like centralisation I grinned to myself. Possibly these things saved time. But I still wondered why somebody should want Alison to go to a place near Mulbery Street.

Almost subconsciously I hastened my steps a little. Candidly, in my heart, I was a little tiny bit worried about Alison. She was a nice girl—one of those rather nice women who work for people like the Old Man, who take a lot of chances, who don't get a great deal of thanks. Women who turn down all sort of propositions just in order to do the *big* job, who miss the chance of meeting men who might make good husbands, who miss all sorts of things, but who just go on doing something that they think they ought to do. Well, I suppose they do it because they like it. I shrugged my shoulders. It seemed to me that I was becoming rather sentimental in my old age.

I stopped in the street and lit a cigarette. I wondered how long I was going to spend my life walking about the streets at night doing odd things, playing it off the cuff. I wondered what it was going to be like when the war was over—when peace broke out. At this moment, as if to give point to the ideas in my mind, the siren went. It shrilled up and down for a minute or so, and two or three minutes afterwards I heard the crash of a flying-bomb. A minute or two after that another one came directly over my head, roaring its way through the night with its tail aflame. I stood watching it, saying a few rather tough things about the Germans. That bomb was going to fall somewhere and where it did fall there was going to be tragedy, injury and death. An indifferent weapon from a military point of view but a very nasty one for those people who were immediately underneath it when it fell.

I turned sharply to the left and entered Mulbery Street. There it was bathed in moonlight looking like any simple village street. One or two of the white houses on the corner where the street curved reflected the moonlight and gave the street almost a Continental touch.

I walked down the street looking to the left and right, trying to find Namur Street. I found it with a peculiar sense of shock. Namur Street was the street into which I had taken White-Face. As I stood there on the corner I wondered . . .

I walked down the street. As I walked, and I was walking quite slowly. I told myself that the idea in my head was of course quite impossible ; that it couldn't be true ; that it was just one of those things that didn't happen. Well, it was possible. It was true and it *had* happened.

I stood outside the door and saw the number of the house in which I'd killed White-Face. It was No. 27. I walked over and tried the door. It was unlatched. I pushed it open. I took the Mauser out of the pocket under my left arm and took off the safety catch. I was feeling lousy. I walked along the passage that led to the back of the house, pushed open the door that led down to the basement, switched on my cigarette lighter. I went downstairs.

The place was absolutely quiet. There was no sound. I stood at the bottom of the stairs with the lighter held above me, the pistol in my right hand, waiting for something. I wasn't quite certain what. I grinned a little to myself. I remembered all the things that I'd done either on my own or with some one else. I told myself that I was becoming rather an old lady these days ; that I was developing nerves.

I put the pistol back into its pocket. I turned and walked along to the place where the packing case was, where I'd left White-Face. It was still there. I walked all round the place looking into odd corners. There was nothing. Then I got it.

I got the big idea. Whoever it was had rung through to Bettina's flat and spoken to Alison was somebody who had wanted me to know, directly or indirectly, that they knew that I'd killed White-Face. They'd sent me back to this place—for what ? I shrugged my shoulders.

I walked back to the end room and pulled the packing

case out. It was heavy. It was difficult to move. I grinned to myself. So White-Face was still there. Maybe I'd been wrong in my supposition. I pulled the packing case round, exerted a little strength and pulled it over on its side. I held up the light and looked inside.

I hadn't been wrong in my supposition! Somebody had taken the trouble to take White-Face out of the packing case. They'd taken the trouble to take White-Face out of the packing case and put somebody else inside. Alison's face—still pretty and relaxed in death—looked up at me from out of the packing case! There was a very neat round hole in her forehead between the eyes. Her eyes were open and they looked frightened. I pushed the packing case back against the wall. I sat on it, lit a cigarette. I sat there in the darkness.

For once in my life I felt very angry. I didn't know why. I hadn't known Alison very well, but she was a good kid.

I don't know how long I sat there. Time doesn't mean very much when one's mind is working as quickly as mine was, but eventually I got off the packing case, stubbed out the cigarette on its top, decided to go home.

The decision wasn't entirely successful. At this moment the cold basement was flooded with light from an electric torch which shone fair into my eyes and bathed the rest of the corner in silvery whiteness. Then a light was switched on. A single unshaded globe produced a light that bathed the white walls of the basement cellar in a peculiar unholy light.

In the doorway stood Bettina Vaile. In her right hand was a Luger pistol which was pointing ominously and quite steadily at my navel.

I got it. I thought a trifle bitterly: Life is full of surprises. Never a dull moment!

She was smiling. And she looked like the devil himself. She said: "Well . . . Michael . . . my dear delightful Michael. My beloved one. Love of my life. I think you and I will have our little talk now. After which we'll see if we can find room in that packing case for yet another one. Even if he is as big as you, my sweet!"

CHAPTER FIVE

SAMMY !

I DID SOME very quick thinking. At least I tried to do some quick thinking. Actually there wasn't anything to think about. The situation was so obvious that it almost creaked. But I summoned up a mental picture of the Old Man. I visualised what he would look like if he could be present at this rather interesting scene. Also I wondered just what he would have to say. Whether he would be able to find words to express his feelings adequately.

I'd been taken for a ride. I thought I was using Bettina Vaile as a superior sort of stooge and she'd very cleverly turned the tables on me. If she didn't finish me off she'd be a fool. But of course she would finish me off. That's what she was here for.

I said : " Well . . . well . . . well, Bettina ! This is a nice little surprise, isn't it ? Just fancy . . ." I smiled at her. " How you must be laughing."

She said : " Of course ! I find the situation very amusing."

I didn't say anything. I looked at her. Now she seemed quite different. I noticed the high-cheek-bones, the peculiar glint in her eyes. There was something almost ferocious in her expression, that peculiar hardness which comes from the exclusive and somewhat peculiar training that all the women in Himmler's External Intelligence groups go through.

I spread my hands hopelessly—but I was still smiling at her. I said : " *Ich gratuliere Ihnen Meine Dame. Sie sind eine sehr gute Schauspielerin. Es wurde mir sehr grosse Freud bereiten den Hals durchzuschneiden !* "

She gave me a charming smile. She said :

" *Was immer der Scherz ist, ich werde vielleicht das Vergnugen haben Ihren durch zuschniiden. Wie werede ich mich freuen. Sie sterben zu sehen—Sie Schweinhund !* "

I shrugged my shoulders. " Well, my delightful Bettina," I said. " So that's that. Now we all understand each other, and all you have to do is to get on with the shooting."

She smiled evilly : " I shall like that," she said. " I've had quite considerable experience in shooting men. I've been wondering just where I shall shoot you. I think in the stomach. It hurts a lot and takes quite a time."

I yawned. I asked : " Is that where you shot Carew ? I suppose it was *you* ? "

She said : " Actually—no. I should have liked to, but I hadn't the honour or the pleasure. That fell to some-one else." She began to laugh. She went on : " I think the situation is most amusing. I followed you down to Dorking, wondered what you were doing on the golf course. And then, if you please, you poor besotted idiot, you had a clever idea about me. Of course I guessed what it was. You thought if you could make my acquaintance the —acquaintance of the so charming Mrs. Bettina Vaile— take me back to London, make friends with me, you'd be able to make use of me. You'd be able to see if your enemies took any interest in Mrs. Bettina Vaile. You hoped, through me to find out who they were.

" I thought it would be a great pity if you were dis-appointed, and you must agree that the ' theatre ' was very good, wasn't it, Michael ? I fired that bullet through the window of my bedroom myself. I knew you'd fall for that one—just as you've fallen this one. Incidentally, you saw what was in the packing case on which you're sitting, didn't you, Michael ? "

Her eyes blazed. She looked like the devil. She went on : " Really, you've been rather unlucky. Things have turned out badly for you." She relaxed, leaned grace-fully against the wall behind her. " Actually, you've never had much of a chance, and I knew that you would believe the story I told you about the unfortunate Alison. I knew that if I told you she had been telephoned for and had gone out you would immediately go after her to see what had happened. And then you would arrive here. You would find that she had been directed to the place where you killed our unfortunate compatriot—(inciden-tally, I'm rather glad about that ; he was so stupid—keen and enthusiastic but not overblessed with brains)—and then your curiosity would be aroused."

She laughed softly. " It was aroused, wasn't it, Michael? When you came here, when you found it was the same house, you were very curious, weren't you ? And then you came in and found your poor little Alison doubled up and pushed into the packing case. Poor sweet. . . . Were you *very* fond of her, Michael ? "

I didn't say anything for a moment. I was thinking just what I would like to do to this woman if I had the chance ; this sadistic harpy who was, at the moment, enjoying herself thoroughly.

Eventually I grinned at her. I was beginning to wonder why she was doing so much talking instead of getting on with the business in hand.

I said : " Well, we break equal now, don't we ? I got your boy friend and you've got Alison Fredericks. That's all right . . . she wouldn't mind—not very much. You see, she was rather a decent sort of girl."

" Meaning, of course, my delightful Michael, that I'm not." She laughed at me, showed her white teeth.

I said : " Listen, stupid . . . before we're through with you you'll have it all right."

She yawned. She said : " *We ?* And who may I ask is we ? Surely you're not counting yourself in on this game any longer, Mr. Kells—the so clever, so courageous, so brilliant, Michael Kells." She shrugged her shoulders. " I must admit it was rather clever of you and Carew to exist for a year in the Pas de Calais as German officers. I must admit that was quite a brilliant exploit. But it seems that you're not quite so ingenious in your own country."

I made up my mind how I'd play this. There was only one way.

" Aren't you taking rather a lot for granted ? " I asked. " Surely you have too much intelligance to think that Carew and I would have been playing this thing on our own. Surely you must realise that it doesn't matter a damn what you do or you don't do ; that you'll eventually win it. Incidentally, you're beginning to bore me. Would you mind if I smoked ? "

She said smoothly : " No, my dear Michael—not at all. But when you put your hand in your pocket take care that you bring out only a cigarette case. I'm a very good shot. I never make a mistake."

I said : " Don't worry about that. I wouldn't shoot you now if I had the chance. I'm going to keep you on ice for a bit."

I took out my cigarette case and lighter, lit a cigarette. I deliberately blew a puff of smoke across the space between us towards her face.

She asked : " I wonder why you think you can talk like that."

I said : " I don't think anything about it. I know."

My certainty seemed to shake her a little bit. She said : " Exactly what do you mean by that ? "

I produced my little fairy tale. I said : " The trouble is that you misjudge people. Alison Fredericks wasn't half such a little fool as you thought. On her way round here she telephoned me. I realised immediately what this place was. I realised this was the place where I'd parked your boy friend. Surely you don't think I just wandered round here casually on my own, do you ? Do you think I'm such a fool as that ? "

She said : " Aren't you ? "

I said : " Listen, I'll take a chance, if you like. At the present moment the barrel of that pistol of yours is pointing somewhere in the region of my navel. If you squeeze the trigger that's the end of me. It's also the end of you because you won't get further than the door of this house. I've a watchdog on the other side of the street. You didn't think I was such a fool as to come here *alone*, did you ? "

She said slowly : " Supposing that what you say is true . . . well, even if it were true you'd be dead and that's the main thing."

I took another chance. I said : " No, it isn't. Not so far as you're concerned. Whilst I'm alive you've got a chance of getting what you want."

She looked at me quickly.

I went on : " You tried to get it from Sammy and you couldn't. You went to all sorts of trouble to try and find out where it was. You couldn't do it. Now you've turned your attention to me. But I won't be any good to you if I'm dead."

She said : " Do you mean to tell me that if I were to spare your life you'd give us what we wanted ? Besides "—she smiled—" even if you did it might not be of any use to us now."

I shrugged my shoulders. I said : " Look, I'm bored with talking to you. Get on with the shooting."

She moved a little. She leaned gracefully against the wall, the arm holding the pistol hanging down by her side. I noticed her feet, placed together firmly—such small feet and such graceful ankles. I found myself wondering how such a so-and-so could be so damned attractive.

She said, with a little, almost quaint, smile : " We'll get on with the shooting when *I* feel like it. I think it's rather nice to listen to you, to let you talk, to keep you in suspense wondering just when I'm going to kill you and just *how* . . ."

" Really," I said. I produced another grin. " So you haven't actually decided to shoot me. You may use some other process ? "

" Why not ? " she asked. She smiled again—that peculiar little smile. She went on : " You had another of your so brilliant agents—a delightful person named Cressy—in Germany. This Cressy was quite pleasant and not at all unclever. Like you and the unfortunate Carew he was there as a German officer. But he had done even better than you, my darling Michael. He had actually, by means of forged papers and a most superb nerve, managed to get himself attached to the Rocket Experimental Stations on the Baltic coast. But *what* an achievement ! It was most unfortunate for him that he slipped up. And in the most extraordinary manner. Would it interest you to hear about it ? "

I did not reply. I thought again that Bettina was wasting a hell of a lot of valuable time in talking about sweet nothing—or was she wasting time ? Possibly she was trying to find out something—some small thing that I might let slip.

I said : " I'm always interested—except when you talk about yourself."

She made a moue. She said : " You do dislike me, darling Michael, don't you ? And you're going to dislike me so very much more before I'm finished with you. Well . . . to return to our friend Cressy who was doing such very distinguished work for you at Peenemunde, one night, there was a very bad air raid. As you know, the R.A.F. had already discovered the existence of the experimental Rocket station and were trying hard to bomb it out of existence.

" Poor Cressy—who was giving a really good performance as a Captain of Heavy Anti-Aircraft—had been on duty for several nights and was very tired. After the raid he was relieved and went to his quarters which were situated in a row of wooden huts with a communicating corridor. He flung himself down on his bed, fully dressed, and went to sleep.

" I was in the neighbourhood. I was looking for another spy—a Frenchman—and I looked into all the sleeping quarters just on the chance of finding him somewhere or other. We knew he was in the neighbourhood.

" Well . . . I opened Cressy's door and looked in. He was sleeping soundly on his bed and apparently dreaming. I was about to close the door and go away with a mental apology for disturbing a German officer's rest, when Cressy began to talk in his sleep—in English. But in *English*, my delightful Michael ! Amusing, is it not ? "

I shrugged my shoulders. So that was how Cressy had won it.

She went on : " Just at this moment the R.A.F. second wave of bombers came in. They made a most fearful din. The thought occurred to me that possibly it would be a good thing for me to execute the English spy on the spot. I intended to shoot him but on second thoughts I came to the conclusion that it would be more amusing to cut his throat. So I did—whilst he was asleep. I was wondering whether I would use the same technique on you."

I said : " You wouldn't find it so easy to cut *my* throat —especially now that I happen to be very wide awake ! "

" I should find a way," she said.

I yawned again—very loudly and rather theatrically. " One thing is quite obvious to me," I said, " and that is that the idea of killing me doesn't appeal to you a bit. First of all for the reason I've already explained, and secondly because quite obviously you haven't found the thing you're looking for—the thing which you think Sammy Carew had and which he hadn't got—the thing which you think it possible I might have. Well . . . I *might* have it, mightn't I ? And I certainly haven't got it on me, so killing me would be a waste of time. You've already decided that, haven't you, my adored Bettina ? So do what you like and damn your eyes. But stop talking because, as I told you before, you bore me."

She moved away from the wall. She came a little closer to me. She said : " You are an English pig-dog and I am going to shoot you in the stomach and I hope you take a very long time to die ! "

It struck me suddenly that she meant what she was saying. The hand holding the pistol came up. There was a flash and a report. The dim bulb of the electric lamp seemed to grow very big and to burst in my face.

I toppled off the packing case and the floor came up and hit me.

When my senses worked sufficiently for me to be able to sit up on the floor and lean against the packing case. I looked at the illuminated dial of my wristwatch and discovered that it was a quarter-past four. I must have been unconscious for over three hours.

I felt the side of my head gingerly. It was cut, but the bleeding had stopped. There was a lump on it like a small Roc's egg. I had the best headache I'd ever had in my life. Luckily nature, which I *thought* had endowed me with a certain amount of common sense, certainly gave me a very thick skull.

There was a peculiar odour hanging about the place— a mixture of carbon-monoxide and something else. I grinned—at myself I'm afraid—at the idea of being put out by a gas pistol—because obviously that was what Bettina had used.

All of which rather supported my theory that she was not at all keen on my being dead—at the moment. That it was necessary that I should, for a time at any rate, remain alive. I wondered why ; concluded that I might concentrate on that point at some other time.

I began to think about Bettina Vaile—or whatever her real name was. I spent quite a time thinking about her and some more time in originating some new oaths which embraced, quite comprehensively, her birth, parentage, life and future.

And I wondered why she had taken the trouble to come round to Namur Street for the express purpose of shooting at me with a gas pistol. There must have been some reason for this. Perhaps she had wanted me out of the way while she pulled something off elsewhere—something with which my presence might possibly have interfered. Bettina and her friends were not the sort of people to stop at murder. They hadn't worried about killing Sammy and Alison Fredericks and they certainly weren't going to worry about killing me. So why hadn't she done it ? I thought possibly I might guess the answer to that one.

I was more than ever certain that the quartet—for it had now become a quartet—consisting of Bettina, Auntie, White-Face and Janine, were very busily engaged in looking for something. They thought originally that Sammy had it. Now they'd concluded that he hadn't. My remark had started something in Bettina's mind. She'd got an idea from somewhere—an idea that if I went on living I'd lead them to what they wanted. I thought it would be very interesting to know just what it was they did want.

After a while I got up. I fumbled around the walls, switched on the electric light switch. When the light went on it took me quite a few seconds to regain my balance. I stood leaning against the wall feeling rather like the Wreck of the Hesperus, wondering what the next move in the game was going to be. But by the time I'd finished my cigarette I came to the conclusion that there wasn't any good to be done by stopping in this cellar working out problems that had no solutions.

I practised walking up and down for a little while in order to find my balance; then I switched out the light, snapped on my cigarette lighter, went up the stairs, out into the street. I stood in the dark street looking at No. 27. Rather a fateful house—No. 27. White-Face had met his Waterloo there and so had that poor kid Alison. I'd realised I'd got to do something about her. At least, the Old Man would have to, which meant that I'd got to tell him that he'd lost another agent. He was going to be even more pleased with that.

I walked home slowly. It was just past five o'clock when I opened the door of my apartments, switched on the light in the hall and wandered across to the bathroom. I bathed my face in cold water and as well as I could examined my head in the looking-glass. It could have been worse. I was lucky not to have a cracked skull.

I went into the sitting-room, crossed to the sideboard and mixed a whisky and soda. I was working the siphon when I saw the large quarto envelope propped up against the back of the sideboard. It was addressed to me in a handwriting I didn't know—unstamped. I opened it. Inside was another envelope enclosed in a note which said :

Dear Mr. Kells,

I found this envelope, unstamped and addressed to you, in a gutter near Mulbery Street. You will notice in the corner is a pencilled request that the finder should post this. I felt that as this letter may be important to you I ought to take it round to your address, and I am leaving it for you with this note.

Yours truly,

James Thwaites.

I put the piece of paper down and picked up the envelope. It was dirty and soiled with mud. It was addressed to me in pencil and written across the corner were the words—" *The finder will be doing a great service if he will post this letter.*"

I got as near to a gasp as I ever got in my life, because, believe it or not, the handwriting was Sammy's.

I drank the whisky and soda ; opened the envelope. Inside were three or four sheets of paper which had obviously been torn from a notebook. I read the note, written in the code shorthand Sammy and I always used :

Dear Micky,

This is a hell of a job, isn't it ? At the present moment I'm in a spot and it doesn't look as if I'm going to get out of it.

First of all a word of explanation. I steered away from you at the party because there was a woman there who I'm rather scared of. I didn't want her to check on any connection between you and me. She was watching me like a cat. I'm not quite certain about it but I think—and I've only instinct to go on— that she is on the other side. I thought the best thing to do was to get good and cut—which I did. I knew in those circumstances you wouldn't even attempt to talk to me. My one idea was to give you my address so that you could get in touch with me so that we might take this matter up later to-day. Well, it hasn't come off.

After I'd left the party—and I think that you enjoyed yourself and will probably want to go there again—I went off to my rooms and mixed myself a hair of the dog that had bitten me. But in the meantime somebody had been at the whisky bottle and my perfectly good whisky had been turned into a first class Micky Finn. I went out like a light. However, the old head-piece seems a little stronger than my friends thought, and I came to, very dizzy and not able to see very well, but well enough to observe a couple of people carefully going over my room. I managed to get up and make a dash for my hand-gun which was under a book on the side table and loosed off a couple of shots hoping that somebody in the house would do something about it. Nobody did and I merely fell over and went out again assisted by a bat over the head from one of my visitors—a most unsatisfactory business.

Incidentally, the reason why I took rooms in Kinnoul Street is that I had come to the conclusion on the day I arrived in this country that somebody was taking a great interest in me—a young gentleman with a white face and a predeliction for make-up. Later I was able to discover that he was staying at the

Kinnoul Street house and so I thought I might as well stay there too. The place is run by a quite nice sort of woman who may be able to tell you something.

When I came to for the second time I found myself in the place where I am writing this note. There is a window in this room, fairly high and barred. I have an idea that I am on a second or third floor. The sound of traffic which I can hear vaguely through the partially opened window seems a long way away.

About the job, which incidentally I have only got wise to during the last twelve hours, one of Himmler's special sections is over here trying to check on the flying bombs. The first ones are apparently not yet out of the experimental stage. They hope to be able to aim these things. *The party over here, in which I believe there are two or three women, has the important job of checking where the bombs come down and getting the information back. Just how they propose to do this I don't know, but there it is.*

I believe that at the party there were at least two or three of these people, so in case you don't remember the address here it is : Mrs. Charles Marinette, 324 Glaston Court, St. John's Wood. If necessary you can have a check up on everybody who was at the party and move from there. The woman I was afraid of, and as I said before this is merely instinct, was a tall, rather too-beautiful woman with blonde hair. When I say too beautiful I mean there was something rather cut and dried about her particular form of loveliness—a kind of tailormade beauty. I expect you'll understand what I mean. She had something very good in the way of figures. I don't know what her name is.

I'm afraid all this isn't going to be of very much use to you but there's just a chance that you may put your finger on something that adds up with some point I've suggested.

I'm not very pleased with the spot I'm in at the moment because I haven't seen any of the people who brought me here, and so I can't tell you anything about them except that they're a tough crowd. You'd better watch your step. Also I'm beginning to think that there was something a little screwy about the Kinnoul Street dump. Not only because I saw the gigolo bloke go there but also it wouldn't have been easy for the boyos who were in my room to get in if they hadn't had some sort of help from the inside. Somebody *in that place must have heard me loosing off my hand gun—unless of course the woman who runs it was out, and I don't see why she should have been out at that time of night—or morning.*

Yesterday I picked up the gigolo fellow again in Kinnoul Street. He was hanging about on the corner of the street. I got into conversation with him and we finished up at a public house called The Heap of Feathers in Mulbery Street. We had a few drinks together. I should say he's very dangerous.

It was through this fellow that I went to the party. He suggested that it might be amusing and, as you know, I'll try anything once.

These idiots haven't been over me yet. Perhaps they feel it doesn't matter! I've still got my notebook and a pencil, and, by a stroke of luck, an envelope. I'm writing this letter to you and I'm going to take a chance and try to throw it between the bars of the window, which is open just a little at the top. Maybe you'll get it, If not—well, so what!

Well, good luck to you, Micky. If I get out of this we'll have a drink together, but somehow I doubt it. I've got an idea in my head that ' I've had it.'

Yours ever,

Sammy.

PS.—I'm working with a very swell woman. She was at the party too. She's got everything, and brains. Her name is Janine Grant and her address is 16 Verity Street.—S.

I poured myself out another whisky and soda and drank it slowly. Then I lit a match and burned Sammy's letter. I felt greatly obliged to Mr. Thwaites—whoever he was!

I lit a cigarette; began to walk up and down the room.

This job had been a hell of a racket from the start. Everybody, including myself, had tried to create situations in which they could get something to start on. Nobody—at least no one on our side, had done any good. I'd been chasing Janine, wasting time on her when, had I known who she was, I might have achieved a great deal by now.

Life was certainly full of surprises.

But now I'd a fairly good idea what had happened. I'd a good idea what had happened to Sammy, to Janine, to Auntie and the whole lot of them. I pieced the story together from the start, filling in such blanks as there were —and there were plenty of blanks, believe me—with guesses.

And I made a plan of campaign. Something had to be done and goddamned quickly, otherwise the Old Man was going to have apoplexy. The first thing was to contact Janine and find out *exactly* what the game had been ; just how Sammy—and Sammy was nobody's fool—had intended to play it and just where she came into the story. That done, I proposed to take Freeby into my confidence and let him know what the job was all about from the start. By doing this he could carry on if Bettina or her friends actually got around to knocking me off.

And I was going to be very careful of Bettina. That piece was damned bad medicine. She was very clever, a particularly good actress, and she would stop at nothing. Bettina was tough all right.

And I owed her one for Cressy. I believed what she had said about him. She killed Cressy all right, *and she knew his real name* as apart from the German one he had been using. Where had she got that from ?

I began to think about Cressy. That boyo had been one of our best people. A superb linguist, clever as paint and with the nerve of the devil.

I remembered the night when Sammy and I—both of us highly respected Junior Officers in a German Rocket Battery in the Pas de Calais—a situation which we had secured by knocking off the two officers who had been sent to the district from the East, whom nobody knew, and whose papers and uniforms we grabbed—first got the idea about Cressy. The senior officer on the Artillery Fire Command—one Meyerein—who was one of the leading rocket experts—came to inspect our group of batteries before leaving for the Peenemunde Experimental Station on the Baltic coast. Directly Sammy and I saw him we looked at each other. He was the very spit of Cressy—the same height, same type of face, same walk.

He stayed four days. But that was long enough to get Cressy over, dropped by parachute, and on the night that the unfortunate Major Meyerein left he had rather bad luck.

Sammy and I upended his car, dealt with the Major, buried him in a wood and fitted out Cressy with his uniform, papers, documents and the whole bag of tricks. Cressy, who spoke German and half a dozen other languages like a native, went up to Peenemunde and had evidently played it off the cuff up there, with a certain amount of success, until Bettina had got wise to him. After which it was curtains for him.

But I'd an idea in my head that he'd got some information over here first ; something which, however nebulous it might have seemed to the ordinary Intelligence boyo, would have meant something to Sammy who knew the background of the job, and Cressy's particularly bright mentality.

On the other hand there was the rather ominous fact that Bettina knew Cressy's name. *How?* Up at Peenemunde they knew him only as Meyerein. He had nothing on him to give him away. How did she know he was Cressy?

I sighed. Maybe they had somebody working over here long before Bettina arrived. Somebody who was wise to Cressy just as they were wise to Sammy and me.

I stubbed out my cigarette. All this, I thought, could wait till to-morrow. I was tired and the idea of bed was inviting.

I went into the bedroom just as the telephone began to ring.

CHAPTER SIX

FREEBY

I STOOD looking at the instrument dubiously. I had had quite enough telephone calls for one evening, and the memory of Bettina's call was still in my mind. I thought maybe somebody else was going to try something on. I picked up the receiver. It was Freeby.

He said : "Sorry to worry you, but I thought you ought to know that Janine hasn't been home."

I said : "I see. And you don't like that ? "

"To tell you the truth I'm not particularly concerned," he answered. "I don't know enough. But I thought you ought to know."

I said : "To tell you the truth I don't think we have to worry about Janine a great deal, but since you're on the line we might as well get one or two things over and done with. I want to talk to you."

He said : "O.K., Mr. Kells."

I asked : "Where are you now ? "

He replied : "I'm at the telephone booth a hundred yards from The Heap of Feathers in Mulbery Street."

"That's fine, Freeby," I said. "Go down to the end of the street past The Heap of Feathers and on the left you'll find a street called Namur Street. Meet me outside No. 27. I'll come right round."

He said all right and hung up.

I lit a cigarette, drank a small whisky and soda, got my hat and went out. I came to the conclusion I might as well make a night of it.

I walked quickly round to Namur Street. It was dawn and a little chilly. I walked quickly, wondering in a vague sort of way why Janine hadn't gone home.

Freeby was standing outside No. 27. He had the same benign and rather disinterested expression on his face. His hands were in his pockets. He looked cold.

I said : "We'll get this over and then you and I might be able to have a few hours in bed. Come inside."

I led the way into No. 27 along the passage down into the basement. I switched on the electric light. I said :
" Sit down on the packing case."

He sat down. I gave him a cigarette.

I asked : " Have you ever met a girl named Alison Fredericks ? "

He said : " Yes, I'm rather stuck on her. I've worked with her twice. She's a nice girl."

I lit my own cigarette. I said : " You mean she *was* a nice girl."

He never batted an eyelid. He said : " What have they done ? Knocked her off ? "

" She's inside the packing case you're sitting on, Freeby," I said. " Mrs. Bettina Vaile is one of the Himmler ' External ' beauty chorus. I had a session with her here last night."

He shrugged his shoulders. " Well, that's how it goes sometimes. I'm sorry about that kid."

I nodded. " So am I. We'll do something about that some time. Last night I fell for it. Mrs. Vaile—I'd like to know what her real name is—telephoned me and said that *I* had telephoned through to Alison and told her to come round here. She knew that I'd come round here immediately myself to see what was happening. I came round. I found Alison's body in the packing case. She'd been shot between the eyes.

" Then the enterprising Bettina arrived and did a big act with a Luger pistol."

Freeby said : " How is it you're alive ? "

I said : " Because she wanted me to stay alive. It was a gas pistol. I was out on the floor here for a long time."

He looked surprised. He said : " That's funny, Mr. Kells, isn't it ? They take the trouble to fog Alison and not you. I wonder why ? "

I said : " I thought of that. They're looking for something."

" I see," said Freeby. He went on smoking quietly. I began to walk up and down.

I said eventually : " Look, this is what I know about this business. Sammy Carew, one of the Old Man's best operatives—maybe you've heard of him—and I were planted in a German Artillery Station on the Pas de Calais. We were fronting as Junior Officers in the German Artillery Rocket Regiment. While we were there we knocked off a German—Major Meyerein—got his uniform and papers, dressed up another of our people —Cressy—and sent him up to Peenemunde on the Baltic Coast to the main German Rocket Experimental Station. Cressy was there for quite a time until somebody got wise to him and finished him. That somebody was Mrs. Bettina Vaile. She told me about it last night."

Freeby pursed up his lips and whistled softly. He said : " This Mrs. Vaile is definitely *good*, isn't she ? She doesn't give a damn about anybody knowing just what she's at. She tells you all about herself and saves you the trouble of finding it. She sounds like the well-known Secret Service agent on the films. I wonder what she's playing at. Anyhow, she's got a nerve. She's pretty good."

I said : " She's damned good. And she knows it. We've got to be careful of that piece." I went on : " The disturbing thing was that she knew Cressy's name."

He said : " That isn't so good, is it ? I wonder how she knew that."

I said : " I don't know. But the fact that she did know his name has given me an idea. Carew and I left the Artillery Station in the Pas de Calais at different times. We got away together but Carew came over first. I was hiding in the woods until I got the tip off. Then I came over. Well, whilst we were serving with the Germans we both had identification certificates and the photographs on those certificates are duplicated at Divisional Headquarters. So when we went they knew there was something screwy. All they had to do was to get those pictures out of the file and get them over here, and their people on this side would know who to look for. Got it ? "

He said : " I've got it."

I went on : Sammy Carew was trying to pick up one of the Himmler External Sections that's over here. This section is trying to check on the flying bombs and rockets they send over, to get back information as to range and where they fall, so that they can start directing these

things instead of shooting them off blindly. Apparently
Carew had nothing to start on, but he had the same idea
as I've just got. He knew they'd have seen his duplicate
photograph ; that if there was anybody over here who
was interested, sooner or later they'd get on to him. So
he just hung around until he found he's got somebody on
his tail—that somebody being a white-faced rat that I
knocked off. You got that ? "

He nodded.

" Carew pulled one on this fellow," I went on. " He
found he was living at Kinnoul Street. That's why he
went and lived there. He was taking some chances, but
he *was* getting next to these people. The day after I
arrived here I was supposed to contact Carew. He told
me to meet him at a party. He was going to this party at
a suggestion made by White-Face, and he had the idea
in his head that White-Face was trying to show him to
some people who were at that party. Sammy got wise
to this. He deliberately got a little drunk, so that I
shouldn't talk to him ; so that he wouldn't give me away
if they weren't already on to me. But candidly I think
he was wasting his time. I think that they were on to
me too. Anyway, I evened it off by getting cut myself
in order to keep the picture right."

He said : " I see. It's fairly simple, isn't it ? "

" Quite simple," I said. " I remembered a woman
who was at that party—this girl Janine. But I made a
mistake about her. She's on our side. She was working
with Sammy. But there was another woman there that
he didn't like—a woman who he describes as being a
beauty in a tailormade sort of way—a fair-haired woman.
I've got an idea in my head who that might be."

He said : " Sorry to interrupt, Mr. Kells, but how do
you know this ? "

I grinned at him. " The voice from the dead," I said.
" I got a letter from Carew to-night. He threw it out of
a window before they killed him and somebody brought
it round."

He nodded. He said : " So they were wise to Cressy,
eventually wise to Carew and wise to you. That's not so
good, is it ? "

I shrugged my shoulders. " Maybe not," I said.
" We'll see."

He went on : " They're probably wise to Janine too."

I shook my head. " I don't think so, Freeby," I said.
" I'll tell you why. When I met White-Face at The Heap
of Feathers I was put in there to meet him. Their idea
was that he should contact me sometime. All right, he
took the trouble to tell me that Carew had gone off with
Janine ; that everybody knew Janine. He suggested that
she was more or less of a tart. Now he wouldn't have
done that if he'd known Janine was working for us,
because he would have known that I should have known
she wasn't. See ? "

He said : " Well, what was the idea ? "

I said : " The idea was a get-out over Carew's death.
The idea was to suggest that the last person who saw
Carew alive was Janine. When I went round to see her
she would naturally play up any story that they'd told
me. She didn't know who I was. She didn't trust
me."

He grinned. " I don't blame her," he said. " When
she's been in this racket a bit longer she probably won't
trust anybody. The longer you're in this game the more
leery you get. Anyhow, she probably didn't know anything about you and she wasn't taking any chance."

I nodded. " I think you're right there," I said. " I've
an idea that what happened on the night of the party
was something like this. Sammy Carew went to the
party and arranged to take Janine with him because he
knew that they weren't wise to *her*. When he got there
he didn't like something about the party or the place or
someone he saw there—probably the good-looking
woman. So he proceeded to turn it into a normal party
so far as he was concerned. He got tight. He knew that
I should realise when I arrived that something was screwy
because he *was* tight. The only contact he made with
me was to slip me a piece of paper with his address on it."

" I get it," said Freeby. " He'd said nothing about
you to Janine. He'd hoped to do that either at the party
or afterwards, but laid off when he got a little scared of
something or somebody."

" That's what *I* think," I went on. " When Sammy saw me drinking a lot of liquor he took that as a tip from me that I was wise to the way he was playing it."

Freeby nodded. " And when the party was over . . . ? "

" When the party was over I believe Sammy went off with Janine," I said. " He saw her home to her place in Verity Street and they had a tail on the pair of them. They knew Sammy had taken her home. He probably left her on the doorstep and went back to his own place. They knew he'd give himself a drink and they'd hocked the whisky or the water bottle. Sammy went out cold, came out of a stupor halfway and found something funny going on. So he fired a couple of shots out of a hand-gun. Nobody took any notice because the only person in the house was playing in too with them. Then Sammy goes out cold again and they take him off some place. When he comes to he writes the letter to me on pages torn from his notebook and slings it out of the window hoping that somebody will get it to me. After that they knock him off and that's that. Have you got all that ? "

" I've got it," said Freeby.

" Then I appear on the scene," I continued. " I go to Sammy's place and the woman with the blue eyes whom I christened Auntie puts me on to The Heap of Feathers because she knows that White-Face is hanging around the neighbourhood. I go into the bar and I ask for Sammy. White-Face gets a big idea. He knows that Sammy saw Janine back to her place the night before so he cleverly tells me that Sammy went off with her only an *hour* before I arrived at The Heap of Feathers. This is going to take me round to Janine's quickly—which it does. Then I hear that Sammy has been killed by a flying-bomb."

I lit a fresh cigarette. " You've got to realise," I went on, " that this White-Face had brains. When they killed Sammy they took him along to the Square to bury him in the place where the excavation's going on. Just as they are about to get busy a flying-bomb comes over and blows one of the trucks on top of Sammy. White-Face or one of his friends finds the nearest policeman and tells him that a man they saw leaving Janine's apartment a few minutes before has been killed by a flying-bomb in the square. This pins Sammy down as having been with Janine immediately before he was killed. In other words it prevents any suspicion of foul play—or at least that was the intention.

"Janine agreed with this story when I first saw her because she was playing for time. She didn't know who the devil I was and she would have said anything to get rid of me. She wanted time to think. Quite obviously, she doesn't know the Old Man or any of his people. She's somebody Sammy picked up spare and she's probably running around the place trying to find someone who is a friend—a *real* friend of Sammy's. But she's afraid to talk too much. She's just hanging around playing it off the cuff."

Freeby stubbed out his cigarette end on the packing case top. He said : "That could be. It all matches up."

"It seems to make sense to me," I said. "But by this time they've got something else to worry about. They've got *me* to worry about. They're wondering what I want with Janine. They guess that I'm trying to find out about Sammy. So they put somebody on *my* tail. They put Bettina Vaile on my tail and she goes after me to Dorking and I try to pull a fast one and scrape an acquaintance, bring her back to town, take her to dinner and do my stuff to see if somebody is going to get on to *her*. She must have been laughing her head off. In the meantime I've made up my mind to have someone keep an eye on her and Janine, so you and Alison come into the thing. You know the rest more or less."

He nodded. "There's one thing I don't get," he said. "If the Vaile woman had kept her head shut and not telephoned you to-night and got you to come round here after Alison you'd never have been wise to her. She could have gone on stringing you along. Why didn't she ? "

"That's an interesting point," I said. "But there might be a reason. Or there might be two. The first would be that she *had* to get me out of the way for a few hours to-night while she pulled something off. She was desperate and she had to do it any way she could. That was the only way she could make certain of me—by getting me round here and knocking me out with that goddam gas pistol."

"That might be it," said Freeby. "And what would the other reason be?"

"Only one thing," I said. "Suppose these people have brought something or other to a head. Suppose they believe that they've got to move quickly and pull off whatever it is they propose to pull off within a matter of days. Well . . . it would be worth while sacrificing somebody to keep us occupied, wouldn't it?"

"I get it," he said. "You mean they'd sacrifice Mrs. Vaile?"

"Right," I said. "You know these people. They'd sacrifice their own mothers to do what they consider to be a good job. Now that Mrs. Vaile has come out into the open and showed me just who and what she is then I'm going to get after her, aren't I? I'm going to get after her with both hands and everything I've got. That's what they *think*."

Freeby nodded. "Yes," he said. "And while you're doing that somebody else—someone you know nothing about—is getting on with the real business. I think that's about it. Not a bad technique either."

He lit a fresh cigarette. "It's a pity about Janine," he said. "I wonder where *she* is."

I shrugged my shoulders. "Wherever she is she's going to turn up some time," I said. "I *hope* . . . Incidentally, there's only one thing to do about this job. We've got to play it the tough way. These people are looking for something. Apart from their own job over here, and the information they're getting back—because the Old Man thinks they're getting it back somehow—there's something they want that they think Carew had. Now they think *I've* got it. That's why Mrs. Vaile didn't finish me off. So they're going to keep on my tail."

He nodded. He said : "It's not going to be very nice for you."

"We must chance that," I said. "The point is we've got to find out who *is* on my tail, because Mrs. Vaile's going to keep out of the way. The white-faced boyo is dead. I know all about Auntie. So somebody new is going to be put in—somebody I don't know."

He said : " I get it. We want to find that person and when we find them . . ."

I smiled at him. I said : " When we find that person, Freeby, we're going to make him talk and he's going to like it."

He got off the packing case. " That suits me," he said. " In the meantime what can I do ? "

" Get everything you can on Mrs. Vaile," I said. " Go round to her apartment and find out anything you can. You'll probably dig up nothing at all—nothing that's worth having. And you might get a line on another woman who was at her party. I've got an idea that this is the woman Sammy was talking about in his letter. The woman who was at the Marinette party. The woman he was scared of."

" What does she look like ? " Freeby asked.

" She's a tailor-made sort of piece," I said. " Beautiful complexion and every hair in its place. Very good clothes—almost *too* good—and a superb figure. About medium height—turquoise eyes—fair hair. Very small feet and walks with a very short and rather affected step. Name—Mrs. Heldon. I don't know where she comes from or anything about her. Your only chance of getting a line on her is if the hall-porter at Mrs. Vaile's place got her a cab and heard her give the man the address. If she used a hired car you may be able to check on it."

Freeby turned round and looked at the packing case. He said : " I'm sorry about Alison. D'you want anything done about that ? "

I said : " Yes. Get in touch with the Old Man and get her moved. Another thing is you might remember that little Bettina will *expect* to have somebody put on her. Your job isn't going to be too safe. They'll probably be on the look out for you."

He grinned. He said : " The same thing goes for you. But I expect they'd rather have *you* than me."

I shrugged my shoulders. " We all get it one day," I said. " You'd better be getting along, Freeby."

He said : " Good-night or rather good-morning, Mr. Kells. I'll be seeing you . . . I *hope*."

I thought I hoped so too.

It was three o'clock and a nice afternoon when I awoke. I got up, bathed, put on a dressing-gown, lit a cigarette and began to walk about the flat. I was thinking about Freeby. I was thinking that it was very possible Freeby might win it just as Alison had won it, but I didn't see what I could do about that.

I began to think about Janine. Just whether she was important or not so far as this business was concerned I had no particular means of knowing. She might be and she might not be. She might know a lot or nothing. In any event I hoped that whatever her nocturnal appointment had been last night, by now she would be at home and ready to talk.

I walked around the place for a quarter of an hour ; then I rang the Old Man. When I heard the ringing tone I wondered what sort of a bawling out I was going to get. But for once I was wrong. He was nice. In fact, he sounded a little too nice to me.

I said : " Good-afternoon. I expect you've seen Freeby by now ? "

He said : " Yes, I've had a talk with him. We're looking after everything. It seems as if things are developing. What do you think of the situation, Kells ? "

I said : " I think I like it just a little bit better. I'm beginning to see a little daylight. But one thing's worrying me—Freeby."

He said : " Yes ? Why ? "

I said : " Well, I think my girl friend knows that I'm going to put Freeby or somebody on her tail. She *must* know that."

He said : " Yes, I think you're right. I rather guessed what she was at by what Freeby told me."

I said : " That lady is busily engaged in drawing a red herring across the trail at the moment. Maybe she thinks I'm going to follow it myself. Possibly she thinks I'll put someone else to look after her."

He asked : " What do you want me to do ? "

I said : " I want you to put somebody on to Freeby and there isn't any particular reason why Freeby should know about it. If he does it might affect his actions. But whoever it is is going to look after Freeby has got to be a very tough egg."

There was silence for a little while ; then the Old Man said : " Did you ever meet a man called Ernie Guelvada ? "

I said : " No. But I've heard a lot about him. He used to work with Kane, usen't he—in Lisbon ? "

" Yes," said the Old Man. " Guelvada's a very tough proposition and in his own way he's particularly clever. He might be of use to you. Anyway, I'll put him on to the Freeby thing and I'll tell him about you. If you want to contact him get in touch with this number." He gave me the telephone number. Then he said : " All right, Well, get on with it."

I heard the receiver click as he hung up.

I thought the Old Man was pretty cute. Ernie Guelvada was just the person for this job. Guelvada was as tough as hell, had a peculiar charm—all his own—and no scruples. He'd worked with Kane, stalking and knocking off enemy agents in Lisbon for years. A very bright one —Guelvada—with a hate for anything German that would be hard to beat. The story was that a Panzer Officer had tortured his girl friend in the early days of the war. She died and after that Ernie had only one idea —killing Germans. He actually *liked* it and took a great pride in his work.

I smoked another cigarette and gave myself a short tot of whisky. Then I dressed, opened up my cabin trunk and went through my collection of identity cards, passports, all the odds and ends that I have collected. I found what I was looking for—a blank Scotland Yard Warrant Card. I filled in the name of Detective-Inspector Summers in the blank space, telephoned through to Guelvada and told him to come and see me at four-thirty, put on my hat and went out.

I walked slowly in the direction of Mulbery Street. Somehow or other I was feeling rather more pleased with things. I had an idea that something would happen—something that would give me a definite lead. After all, Janine had to know *something*. She couldn't have been toting around on this job with Sammy in a complete state of ignorance, and directly she knew who and what I was she would talk.

Incidentally, I was rather pleased with the idea of seeing her again. Janine, I thought, was a rather exciting person, and I was more than pleased that she was playing on our side.

It was a bright afternoon and I found myself feeling almost light-hearted as I passed The Heap of Feathers in Mulbery Street. I looked down the little passage that led to the saloon bar as I went past and thought that life was a strange proposition. I wondered what the people who were in the bar on the night that I met White-Face would think if they knew what had happened in their quiet and salubrious neighbourhood.

When I got to 16 Verity Street I pressed the housekeeper's bell and waited. Two or three minutes afterwards the door opened. Inside, a rather neat, plump, grey-haired woman of about fifty stood looking at me enquiringly.

I said : " Good-afternoon. You're Mrs. . . . ? "

She said : " Mrs. Adams. What can I do for you ? I'm afraid all my apartments are full."

I said : " I'm not looking for apartments, Mrs. Adams." I produced the Warrant Card and showed it to her. " I'm Detective-Inspector Summers of Scotland Yard," I said. " I believe there's a lady called Janine living in the house."

She looked at me. Her eyes were astonished. She said: " Yes, that's right. Do you want to see her ? "

I said : " If you please. I suppose she's in ? "

She said : " I don't know. Two gentlemen from the Civil Defence came round to see her about ten o'clock this morning. Whether she's gone out since I don't know."

I said : " Tell me something, Mrs. Adams, when the gentlemen from the Civil Defence came did they ring her bell or yours ? "

She said : " They rang my bell."

I said : " I see. They didn't tell you, possibly, that they'd been ringing her bell first and got no reply ? "

She said : " No, they didn't say anything like that. They just said they wanted to see her." She looked vaguely uncomfortable.

I smiled at her. " Don't worry, Mrs. Adams. It's nothing very important. What did you tell them to do ? Did you show them up ? "

She said : " No, sir. I was busy. I told them to go up and knock on her sitting-room door."

I said : " Excellent. All right, Mrs. Adams. Had you ever seen these two gentlemen from the Civil Defence before ? "

She said : " No, I hadn't. I thought possibly they were two new ones. I know most of our own people."

I nodded. I said : " I expect they were two new ones. Do you mind if I go up and speak to Miss Janine ? "

She said : " Certainly not. It's on the first floor. Knock on the door on the left of the landing."

I went up the stairs. I knocked on the sitting-room door, but there was no answer. When I tried the door I found it was locked. It took me two or three minutes' quiet work to unlock it ; then I opened the door and stepped into the room.

It looked as if the battle of Hastings had taken place there. The furniture was all over the place. Drawers had been pulled out. The whole place was in disorder. Even cushion covers had been ripped open. I sighed. It seemed as if the two gentlemen from the Civil Defence had had a field day. I stood in the corner of the room looking at the chaos.

Then I walked quietly across the landing and tapped still more softly on the bedroom door. There was no reply and that door was locked. I got it open, went inside. The scene was very much the same. The bedclothes had been thrown back and two or three rather nice evening frocks were flung across the bed.

I lit a cigarette. It was a nice bedroom. Janine had evidently had a pretty taste in arranging things. I thought she'd been rather annoyed if she could see it now. I had an idea in my head that she had not been there when the two men had called. I had an idea that she'd not been back at all last night. Quite obviously, they'd gone over the place—searched it from top to bottom, taken the keys from inside the doors, locked them from the outside and taken the keys away. I thought that it was more than possible that Janine had been very lucky not to be there. I walked about the room looking into odd corners. I didn't know what I was looking for, but I hoped I might find something. I found nothing.

I went back into the sitting-room and looked about the place. There was a writing desk in the corner. I went over to it. On the desk was a blotter. I took out the sheaf of blotting paper and looked between the leaves. There wasn't anything much except an unused postcard. The picture postcard was one of those that you buy in series and this apparently was a country house series. It was a photograph of the Old Moor Lodge at Chippingfield.

I put it back between the leaves of the blotter and continued to wander about the room, trying to find some incongruity—something that somebody had forgotten or dropped. There wasn't anything, but as I turned towards the door I saw a new A.B.C. railway guide on the mantelpiece. I picked it up and held it between two fingers and the thumb of each hand, at the bottom and the top of the binding. I held it up above my head. The book opened. I put my finger in the opening, put the book on the mantelpiece. It had opened at a page which gave the train service to Chippingfield, because that was the only place at which the book *had* been opened. I closed the book, put it back in its original position. I took a flying look round both rooms, locked the doors again with a skeleton key on my bunch of keys ; then I went downstairs.

I went to the top of the basement stairs and called Mrs. Adams. When she appeared I said : " Oh, Mrs. Adams, Miss Janine is not in. I think it may be some little time before she's back. The doors of both her rooms are locked. The best thing will be for you not to disturb anything until she comes back."

She said : " Oh . . . you think she will come back, sir ? "

I said : " Oh yes, she'll come back all right. Is the rent paid ? "

" Only to the end of the week," she said.

I asked her what the rent was. She told me. I took out my note case, gave her some notes. I said : " There's the rent till the end of the month, Mrs. Adams. She'll be back by then—I hope."

I walked home slowly. So far as I could see there was only one thing to be done. Anyhow I've always liked the country.

I began to wonder what the hell Janine was at. But I was kidding myself. I knew what she was doing. And I hoped *she* did !

CHAPTER SEVEN

THE GREAT RAVALLO

ERNIE GUELVADA came round at half-past four. An immaculate neat figure, with small feet and a personality that was electric enough to be disturbing. He was on the short side and seemed a little plump at first glance. He only *seemed* plump—in effect he was anything but. Most of it was muscle. He put his feet on the ground with an odd precison usually associated with members of the cat family. His face was round, pleasant, apparently good-humoured. He had a mobile and well-cut mouth. His eyes were of a peculiar steel blue colour. Killer's eyes.

A tough proposition—Guelvada.

He spoke a queer sort of English with the merest trace of a Belgian accent. He was a fan for American gangster films and interlarded his more pedantic utterances with occasional splashes of United States slang which gave his conversation a weird incongruity. The word " hey," used as a sort of full stop, was thrown in at any time that the enterprising Ernie thought of it.

When I'd given him a drink, he leaned up against the sideboard in my sitting-room and regarded the perfect creases in his trousers with equanimity.

110

He said :

"I should tell you, Mr. Kells, that I am very pleased to be working with you—goddam delighted—indeed. I've heard a great deal about you. I believe you don't stand any nonsense. Hey ? "

I said : "You don't like people who stand for nonsense, Guelvada ? "

He said : "From Germans—no." When he said the word "Germans" his hands twitched in a rather peculiar way. He gave me the impression that he wanted to get his fingers round somebody's throat ; that he was a pent up dynamo charged with a great deal of concentrated spleen.

He said : "I personally have never stood for any nonsense from accursed Germans—hey ? "

I said dryly : "I've heard that. Well, maybe you're going to get some fun."

He said : "Nothing would please me better."

"At the same time," I pointed out to him, "don't go running ahead of yourself. Don't let that natural inclination to deal with Germans in the toughest possible way obscure your vision."

He said : "I assure you I'm always extremely smart ! What do I do ? "

I said : "The position so far as you're concerned is perfectly simple. You know Freeby ? "

He nodded.

"I've put Freeby as a tail on a woman called Mrs. Bettina Vaile," I said. "Mrs. Bettina Vaile is a German. She's a member of one of the Himmler External Sections. She's a lady who has deliberately stuck herself under my nose in order that I shall concentrate most of my attentions on her."

He nodded. He said : "That is an old trick. She is to be the red herring while somebody does the work— somebody that you *don't* know."

I said : "That's how it looks to me. I've put Freeby on to her. She'll probably get wise to the fact. She may want to try something funny with Freeby ; possibly somebody else is going to knock *him* off. Your business is to keep an eye on him and the situation in general."

I gave Guelvada an outline of what had happened up to date.

He said : " I understand perfectly."

I took a piece of paper. I wrote down the Bettina Vaile address, one or two other points that I thought he ought to know. I gave it to him. I said :

" Learn those things off and destroy the note. Keep in touch with me here. I think it might be an idea if you telephoned me twice a day. The first time at twelve o'clock in the morning and then again at nine o'clock at night. Even if I'm not here I can get at you through the hall-porter."

Guelvada said : " I think that would be very good."

" Something's going to pop pretty soon," I told him. " That's obvious. Mrs. Vaile didn't bother to come out into the open just to advertise who she was. She knows I'm going to get after her with both hands. She's prepared for that. The main thing is, however, that she wouldn't have done it unless she considered that whatever job she's been on is just about coming to the boil. She's taking a chance against time—and us."

He said : " I think you are quite right. She is a little in a hurry and she thinks that she can get away with it— or someone else can—the goddam frail. Probably the lady is one of those fanatical bitches that prefer to die for the Fuehrer. She thinks you will finish her but while you are doing it someone else will succeed with the big business."

I gave him another drink. I said : " Good luck, Guelvada. Use a gun or a knife or whatever it is you do use if you've got to. But don't do it just for the fun of the thing."

He said : " Very well, Mr. Kells. Thank you very much. I assure you I shan't unless I have to. Good-afternoon."

He looked at the paper casually, brought a little gold lighter out of his pocket, lit the corner of the sheet of quarto paper, watched it burn. He put the ash carefully in my wastepaper basket. Then he picked up his hat, put his heels together, made an almost imperceptible bow and went out. Most of the time that he'd been in the room I'd felt vaguely uncomfortable. He had that sort of nervous disposition. But I liked him. He was the right man for this job.

Thinking about him I concluded I'd much rather be on *his* side.

It was six-thirty and a very beautiful summer's evening when I arrived at Chippinsfield. I parked the car and regarded the small straggling village, which consisted mainly of one street with clusters of detached cottages. After a while I lit a cigarette, walked down the High Street and went into the small hotel. I ordered a whisky and soda ; asked to borrow the local telephone directory.

I sat in the small saloon bar with the telephone directory on my knee and the glass in my hand. I wondered if I was going to be lucky.

I opened the book at " C " ran my finger down the page. When I found it I drank the whisky and soda. There was only one Carew in Chippinsfield—Miss Eleanor Carew. And she lived at Old Moor Lodge. I heaved a sigh of relief. I put the glass back on the bar, went out of the hotel, began to walk down the street.

The village policeman standing on the corner told me where Old Moor Lodge was. On my way I wondered what sort of reception I'd get. I wondered if even now, supposing my guess had been right, I was going to throw out. I came to the conclusion I'd soon know.

Old Moor Lodge was a delightful old house standing in its own grounds. There was an air of peaceful antiquity about it that pleased me. In my mind's eye I could see it as a background for Sammy. I wondered when he'd been there last.

I pushed open the iron gate, walked up the overgrown carriage drive, rang the bell. It was one of those old-fashioned bells that clang for several minutes after you pull it. After a bit the door opened. A very charming old lady, in a grey alpaca frock with a lace fichu, stood in the hall. She looked at me with a pair of twinkling eyes from behind horn-rimmed spectacles.

I said : " Are you Miss Carew ? "

She said : " Yes." She stood there smiling, looking almost as if she'd expected me.

I said : " Forgive me for asking questions. I'll tell you why in a minute. I take it that you're Sammy Carew's aunt ? "

She said : " Yes. I am Sammy's aunt." But she didn't seem surprised at the question. I didn't like that.

I said : " I wonder if I could come in for a minute and talk to you."

" By all means," she answered. She held the door open, and I went into the cool dim hallway. She closed the door behind me, led the way down the passage and into a well-furnished sitting-room. She said : " Won't you sit down ? You'll find cigarettes in that box on the table."

I took a cigarette and sat down. She placed herself in the big chair opposite me.

Miss Carew said very quietly : " Now, what can I do for you ? "

I said : " The situation's a little difficult, Miss Carew. My name is Kells—Michael Kells. I am a very old friend of Sammy's. I suppose you wouldn't have any idea what he's been doing for the last few years ? "

She said with a smile. " I've a perfectly good idea. Sammy's always been in the Army—in the Artillery. He's a Gunner."

I said : " I see." So that was that ! I went on : " The point is that Sammy had an accident not very long ago. I'm trying to find out one or two things about it. It's a rather strange mixed-up story, Miss Carew, and I won't bother you with it."

She said : " Thank you very much. But what *is* it that you want, Mr. Kells ? "

I thought it was no good beating about the bush. It was quite obvious to me that Sammy's aunt was very cool, very intelligent. She wasn't an old lady whom you could take for a ride.

And it was all the tea in China to a bad egg that she knew all about Sammy. She knew what he'd been doing. She *must* have known. Sammy had said that he always stayed with her between trips and she would have guessed anyhow that Gunner Officers don't get up to the stuff Sammy was always at in war time.

He'd asked me once to go down and meet her. I wished I had. She'd have known me. As it was I'd a definite idea she didn't like me a bit. And I didn't blame her. I'd have felt the same.

I said briefly : " I want to know if a very good-looking young woman who sometimes calls herself Miss Janine has been down to see you."

She asked : " Mr. Kells, why should this Miss Janine want to see me ? "

I said : " I'll tell you. She and Sammy were working together on a little assignment—a sort of job that Sammy was doing in addition to his work as an Artillery Officer. I've got an idea that he's disappeared temporarily, and that she might want to know where she could find him, or alternatively how she could get in touch with the people he's working for. It occurred to me, Miss Carew, that she might have heard about you from Sammy ; that she might have come down to see you—to ask you if you knew who Sammy's employers were so that she could make contact with them."

She smiled at me. It was a benevolent smile. She said : " But I don't understand, Mr. Kells. I don't understand what you mean by Sammy's employers. Sammy is an Army Officer. I've told you that."

I thought : It isn't any good beating about the bush. We'd better get down to hard tacks.

I said : " Miss Carew, Sammy was an Army Officer, but for the last three and a half years he's been doing what is usually called special assignment work with me. Well . . . he disappeared some days ago, and I don't like it. In point of fact "—I dropped my voice a little— " I shouldn't be surprised if he were dead. I don't know a great deal about this young woman who calls herself Janine, but I do know that she was a friend of Sammy's. I've lost touch with her. I want to find her. I thought it possible that she might have come here. Has she been here ? "

She said : " Mr. Kells, you understand that I don't

know anything about you. You will also understand that there is no particular reason why I should trust you. I think you're labouring under a misapprehension."

I raised my eyebrows. I wondered what was coming now.

She said : " You're quite mistaken about Sammy being dead. I know he's not dead. He was speaking to me only yesterday on the telephone."

I asked : " Miss Carew, are you sure it was Sammy ? "

She said : " Mr. Kells, Sammy—and if you knew anything about him you would know this—had a most distinctive voice. Do you think I don't know my own nephew's voice. As for this Miss Janine that you talk about, I really don't know anything about her."

I realised that I'd had it. I got up, stubbed the cigarette out in the ash-tray. She was lying all right, and I could guess why, but it wasn't any good talking.

I said : " Well, Miss Carew, thank you very much. I'm sorry you can't help me. I'll be getting along."

She said : " I'm sorry too. Good-bye, Mr. Kells."

She led the way along the passage through the hall and opened the door. As I went through she said with the slightest touch of sarcasm in her voice : " Good evening, Mr. Kells. I'm sorry you have had so much trouble for nothing." She closed the door.

I walked down the carriage drive using some very bad language. Somebody had got at Sammy's aunt. And they'd told her a damned good story. Whoever it was had telephoned her and given such a good imitation of Sammy had fixed *me* all right. They'd guessed I might come along. They probably knew I'd be along to find out about Janine and they'd got in first.

I walked back to the hotel and drank another whisky and soda. The situation was not so good.

Obviously, by now, they were wise to Janine. And I didn't like that at all.

I sat around in the saloon bar for half an hour until nearly half-past seven, drinking whisky, smoking cigarettes and not feeling particularly happy about anything.

The situation did not look so good, but then situations seldom did look really good in my business.

I concluded it was no good sitting down on the job. I walked over to the bar ; indulged in a little conversation with the landlord. I discovered the next town was a place called Walling—a small place five or six miles away off the main road. I walked back to the car, started her up, drove along the Walling road. I was thinking about Janine.

It seemed pretty obvious to me that whoever had put the telephone call through to Sammy's aunt on the day before would have done it from Walling. That was the logical place. They wouldn't try it from Chippinsfield. Of course there were about a thousand other places they could have done it from and even if the call had emanated from Walling I didn't see what good I was going to do. But there was just a chance that I might pick up something in Walling. In any event I didn't see what else was to be done at the moment. I had a pretty good idea what Janine had done ; also I had a pretty good idea as to what was going to happen to that lady if somebody didn't do something fairly quickly. One of these fine days we were going to find little Janine with a happy smile on her face and her throat cut from ear to ear. *Unless* somebody got moving quickly. But how ?

When I got there I put the car up in a garage and had a look round. It was a nice little town, about the size of Dorking, with one big High Street with old world houses and shops on each side and narrow side streets leading off it. There was definitely an atmosphere about the place.

I went into the main hostelry—an old-fashioned inn in the middle of the High Street—because that was the obvious place to go to. The bar parlour—an oak-beamed room, heavy with smoke and a buzz of conversation—was filled with the sort of people who congregate in such a place on market day. I ordered myself a drink and carried the glass over to the leaded window. It seemed to me that I had as much chance of getting wise to anything in Walling as I had of flying straight up to heaven. In fact I had seldom known myself to be so depressed.

There was a vacant space on the other side of the road opposite the window I was looking through and through it I could see the hills in the distance. It was a fine evening and the sky was lovely behind the hills. I found myself wondering why I should consider myself entitled to indulge in these poetic thoughts.

And then it happened.

Out of a tobacconist shop on the other side of the road came Auntie. Auntie—with her trim figure, her sparkling blue eyes, her staccato walk. Auntie, who'd been Sammy's landlady at Kinnoul Street ; who had blinded me with a pepper-pot !

I gulped down the drink and slid out of the hotel quickly. I went after her on the opposite side of the road, keeping well behind people walking on the pavements. I knew that if Auntie saw me just once it would be all over.

She did not even look round. She was walking definitely with an object. She was going *somewhere*. I crossed the road and hastened my steps, coming up close behind her. Luckily there were a lot of people in the street and as I have said she never turned her head. We came to a spot where the main street narrowed, where the crowd was a little thicker. Then I lost her. One moment I saw Auntie and the next moment she was gone. She seemed to have disappeared into thin air. When I got just beyond the place where last I'd seen her I found a narrow alley. I walked down it. There was another small passage running at left and right angles to the alley at the top. She might have gone either way but there was no sign of her.

I came back to the main street, lit a cigarette and cursed. It was obvious that she *must* have gone into some place, but where she'd gone I had not the remotest notion. I walked down the street. Fifteen yards or so beyond the alleyway was a small cinema theatre—the sort of small place that was built thirty years ago and still manages to be popular. I stood outside looking at the board advertising the week's attractions. It occurred to me that there was just a chance that Auntie had decided to go and see the movies, although I didn't see why—

occupied as she was with other matters—she should be interested in the cinema.

I bought a seat and went in. The place was small and musty inside, the projection was not too good and the film was old-fashioned. When my eyes got accustomed to the half darkness I peered about me, trying to find Auntie, but there was no sign of her.

The film ended. The lights went up and I was about to get to my feet and go out when the cinema screen ascended, the curtains behind it opened and the house lights went out. A lady appeared on the stage with some trained doves and proceeded to put them through their paces. Quite obviously there were one or two vaudeville turns included in the evening's entertainment. I sat there looking at the turn on the stage. She was quite good. She made the doves do all sorts of interesting things and they seemed to like it. When her turn ended the tabs came down to perfunctory applause. I got up from my seat, began to walk up the aisle towards the exit. I'd almost reached it when a voice from the stage said: "Ladies and gentlemen, I will now imitate for you the cooing note of the doves you've just heard in Mlle Leclerq's brilliant performance."

I turned round. The tabs had gone up again and on the stage was a man. He was giving an imitation of the cooing of the doves. It was very good.

A yard or so from me stood an usherette. I said to her: "Who is he?"

She said: "That's The Great Ravallo. Our top of the bill this week. You'd think he'd be able to get better jobs than this. You'd think he'd be on a bigger circuit, wouldn't you?"

I said: "Maybe."

Ravallo went on with his turn. He imitated all sorts of noises. He gave an imitation of a man with no roof to his mouth. The audience, rather bored by the previous turn, applauded vociferously.

I took my cigarette case out of my pocket and stood lighting a cigarette, leaning against the wall, watching him. I said to the usherette: "I think he's very good. When does he come on again?"

She said : " During the last show to-night—at about ten-fifteen. We finish the show with him."

I talked to her for a few minutes ; then I went out of the cinema, turned back and walked along the High Street until I came to the passage where I'd missed Auntie. I walked down it. I took the turning at the left at the top. Ten or twelve yards down the passage I found what I was looking for—the stage entrance of the cinema. I walked back to the inn ; ordered another whisky and soda.

I was feeling considerably better. When I took the glass back to the bar I asked the barmaid where the telephone was. She told me. I went in, asked for the number of my apartment in town, spoke to the hall-porter. When he came on the line I said :

" Mr. Guelvada—Mr. Ernie Guelvada—will be tele-phoning me to-night at nine o'clock. I want you to give him a message. You'd better get your pad and write it down."

I waited till he came back with the pad. I went on : " Tell Mr. Guelvada to get himself a car, to come down to Walling in Berkshire, and meet me in the saloon bar at the Crown Inn in the High Street. Tell him I shall be waiting for him at nine-forty-five, so he'll have to move quickly."

I made him repeat the message ; then I hung up. I went back to the bar and bought another drink. I felt I was going to need it.

When I'd finished the drink I went out into the High Street and, walking on the side of the road opposite to the Cinema, approached that building. When I was opposite the passage I shot quickly across the road, down the passage and took the turning to the right at the top.

The turning was a small alleyway curving off to the west of the town and becoming wider in the process. Five minutes' walking brought me to the edge of a golf course. I skirted this and found a small country road with straggling cottages and bungalows dotted along it, or standing back in the fields. Another five minutes and I discovered a small cottage with a " To Let " sign in the overgrown garden. I slipped round to the back and put in a little work on the kitchen door with a bunch of keys. Then I stepped inside.

The place was ideal. It was unfurnished and consisted of three rooms and a kitchen. One room between the front room and the kitchen had a small window looking out across the fields.

I went out through the kitchen door. I closed the door but did not lock it. I walked down the road for some distance and then began to work back towards the town and the High Street, keeping to odd lonely roads where possible. The one thing that scared me was that, just at this moment, Auntie might catch sight of me and ruin the whole performance that I had in mind.

When I arrived back in the safety of the saloon bar at The Crown I heaved a sigh of relief.

Ernie Guelvada walked into the bar at The Crown at twelve minutes to ten. He was wearing a tweed suit, brown shoes, a rather nice thing in green wool shirts and a russet tie. Definitely attired for the country. With the time it had taken him to get into that rig allowed, he must have driven like the devil.

I bought some drinks and we went and sat in the corner.

He said : " I got your message and I scrammed like hell. As you see I waited merely to dress appropriately. I imagine that something has broke—hey ? "

" You imagine right," I told him. " Auntie has broke as you call it. She's here. And she's not here for her health either."

He took out a neat cigarette case, offered it to me, lit our cigarettes. " I find myself goddam interested," he said softly.

" The girl Janine did not go home last night," I told him. " And that was lucky for her too. They went over her apartments—every damned thing was turned inside out and taken apart. When I went there to look round I found a picture postcard under the blotter—a photograph of The Old Moor Lodge at Chippinsfield—a village near here. They'd seen it too. . . . "

Guelvada nodded. " So . . ." he murmured. " And the girl Janine. Where was the doll Janine ? "

" She'd gone down to The Old Moor Lodge to see Sammy Carew's aunt," I told him. " She was trying to find out who Sammy was working for. She knew she was on the top line and she hadn't a lot of time to spare. But they'd got on to that job too. Just how I don't know, but they had. By the time she arrived there somebody had telephoned through to Sammy's aunt and put up a damned good imitation of Sammy. This person said he was Sammy and that when the girl came down and asked questions she was to be put on to so-and-so at so-and-so, but that she was not to be told that it was Sammy speaking. You understand ? "

Guelvada nodded. " Clever," he said. " Quite clever. . . ."

" The old lady was also warned against me," I went on. " They told her that I should probably be around trying to pull something and that I was bad medicine. She wouldn't play with me at all. She wouldn't tell me a goddam thing."

He shrugged his shoulders. " That is always the way with these goddam mommas," he said. " They do one of two things. They either never stop talking at all at a time when one desires peace above all things, or else —if it is desired that they shoot the works—they keep their goddam traps so tightly buttoned up that it's nobody's business. To hell with Miss Carew—hey ? "

I said : " Never mind her. Finding Auntie down here was a bit of luck—if it holds."

He raised his eyebrows. " Jeez ! " he said. " So you have found Auntie—the lady of the pepper-pot—by accident. But how excellent. Let us bounce holy hell out of the old so-and-so—hey ? But how lucky you have been . . . but they told me you were always a very lucky man. The same thing applicates itself to me very often."

" We're going to need all the luck I can get," I said. " But I *was* lucky. I came over here from Chippinsfield on chance and saw Auntie. I lost her down the street near an alleyway that ran to the stage door of a small cinema down the road. There are a couple of turns playing there—vaudeville turns—and one of them is a fellow called Ravallo who imitates voices. . . ."

Guelvada said : " My God ! I am very moved. I am almost excited. A nice piece of luck, hey ? "

" A piece of cake," I said. " This is the boy who put the fake call through to Miss Carew. Auntie has been along to-night to see him. She disappeared into the stage door and was probably sitting in his dressing-room whilst I was watching the performance. You get the implication, don't you ? "

Guelvada said : " I don't quite understand . . . what implication ? Please to be a trifle more explicit . . . hey ? You mean that Auntie—the woman who kept the Kinnoul Street house—paid this man to telephone through to Miss Carew and imitate Sammy's voice. You mean . . ."

I interrupted : " Use your head. This Ravallo couldn't imitate the voice of someone he'd never heard, could he ? "

" My God ! " said Guelvada. " So this was one of them. This——"

" Right," I said. " This was one of the boyos who knocked Sammy off. The only place this Ravallo could have met Sammy was at the place they took him to after he'd been doped. Probably Ravallo was one of the two men Sammy talked about—the two people who were searching his room when he came out of the Micky Finn the first time."

" I comprehend," said Guelvada. " I comprehend perfectly. Something, I feel, should be done to this imitator of voices. And it should not be done too quickly. It should be . . ." He waved his hand in the air expressively.

" There's quite a lot of time for that," I said. " But in the meantime there's some work to do."

" You mean ? " Guelvada looked at me curiously.

" He's going to talk," I said. " He talked on the telephone for Auntie, and now he's going to talk for me—and like it."

Guelvada began to laugh. It was one of the softest, nastiest laughs I had ever heard. It made my spine crawl.

He said : " Excellent . . . most excellent ! I have some very, very good ways to make people talk. With my ways they always talk. You'd be surprised ! "

I said I shouldn't.

He stubbed out his cigarette. " When does one go to work, please ? " he asked.

" We've lots of time," I said. " Ravallo goes on to do his last turn at ten minutes past ten. His act takes about twenty minutes—the girl at the cinema tells me he plays it a little longer in the last performance. After that he's going to change and take his make-up off. That brings us to about ten-forty-five. He'll leave at about ten-forty-five and it'll be fairly dark then. We'll move over there at ten-thirty and find a spot to park in the alleyway."

" I am certain that you have the whole thing organised in an extremely big way," said Guelvada. " I await practical developments with a helluva lot of interest."

He lit a fresh cigarette ; then he said casually—too casually : " Tell me please about this Janine. I am *very* interested. You have probably heard that I am an extremely great lover of women. Like hell ! I should like to hear some more about Janine."

I grinned at him. I *had* heard about him. I said : " She's marvellous. She's got everything, if you know what I mean. Voice, hair, figure—everything is right. *And* she has a great deal of what they call allure—you know the thing the Americans call ' what it takes.' She moves gracefully. It's a treat to watch her walk. A unique person—Janine."

He sighed. " I can hardly wait," he said softly.

I said : " Don't let it worry you."

He looked at me sideways. He said : " Just my goddam luck. Here is the most appealing lady waiting round the corner and my boss arrives on the job first. Not so good. Still "—he shrugged his shoulders—" she may be dead by now—who knows ! In which case everybody will be disappointed."

He sighed again. He went on : " There was a woman in Lisbon. Of the most exquisite beauty, charm and deportment. Some baby, I'm telling you ! I was working over there with Kane, and it became necessary that I contact this lady in order to get some information. Her name was Marandal."*

He sighed even more heavily. " I did not look forward to the interview with her," he continued. " I did not look forward to the interview because I had parted from her a year or so before under somewhat distressing circumstances——"

I looked at my wrist-watch. It was twenty-past ten.

Guelvada said : " I discovered that my so sweet Marandal was not being entirely faithful to me ; that she permitted herself to be necked by some goddam Portuguese—merely because he had a great deal of jack and bought her very valuable diamonds. Therefore I left her. Also, on leaving her I took some of the ice— her diamond necklace and bracelet—with me. She discovered this after I had gone. You will realise, Mr. Kells, that it was very, very difficult, for me to renew this friendship ? "

" It must have been damned difficult," I said. " What happened ? "

" She was working with a Spanish *agent* called Roccas. He was working for the Germans in Lisbon. Kane ordered me to get at him through her. One morning early I went to her villa and found her—at five-thirty in the morning, if you please—playing patience. She looked wonderful. First of all she hit me across the face with a china vase—you can still observe the goddam scar—hey ? After which she attempted to kill me with an antique scimitar. However——"

I said : " The story will keep, Guelvada."

He saw me looking at my watch. He said cheerfully : " So . . . so we go to work, hey ? "

I nodded. We got up together.

" Yes," I said. " Let's take him. And remember this is neck or nothing."

He grinned at me as we moved across the room. He said : " With Guelvada it is never nothing. Never. Indubitably not. No, Sir . . . not on your goddam life ! "

* *Dark Duet.*

CHAPTER EIGHT

GUELVADA

FROM where I was standing in the alleyway—about twenty yards from the stage door of the cinema—I could hear the Panatrope, or whatever they call it, playing *God Save the King*. I stubbed out my cigarette and leaned back into the shadow of the wall.

I was stationed on the town side of the stage door; Guelvada, out of sight from where I stood, lurked somewhere along the other end of the alley on the road to the fields.

Ten minutes or so went by and one or two people came out of the stage door and disappeared into the narrow turning that led to the High Street. Another five minutes went by.

I began to be scared. It occurred to me, suddenly, that The Great Ravallo might be one of those performers who prefer to leave a theatre by the front entrance. If this was so it wasn't going to be so good.

I was chewing over this proposition when I heard the folding door of the stage door entrance bang, and Ravallo came out. He was tall, well-made, and walked with the same swagger that he used on the stage. Outside the stage door he stopped to light a cigarette; then began to walk away from me towards the High Street turning. I went after him quietly.

He was about at the turning when Ernie Guelvada came out of a doorway. I heard him say : " Forgive me, please, but I would be most grateful if you could give me a light."

Ravallo said something, fumbled in his coat pocket. I came up behind him and pushed the barrel of the Mauser —inside my right hand jacket pocket—into his side.

I said : " Come on, Ravallo. Let's have a little talk. Don't be funny. You'd be surprised if you knew how *very* tough we can be."

Guelvada said in German : " How very surprised you would be to know ! "

The man Ravallo did not seem to be fearfully perturbed. He looked from me to Guelvada. He shrugged his shoulders, almost imperceptibly. He gave me the impression of being a little bored with the whole business. He probably was. He might easily have been wondering just how we'd got on to him, or what he was going to do, or what his own particular boss would say or do when he heard that Ravallo had slipped up. Most of the people who work for Himmler are like that. Death doesn't mean an awful lot to them. They don't *like* it, of course, but if it's for the Fuehrer they don't appear to mind too much.

Guelvada was on the right side of Ravallo. He asked : " Where to ? "

" Straight down the alleyway," I said. " There's an empty cottage that will do nicely. It's not far."

" Excellent," said Guelvada. " Let us go."

We began to walk. The Great Ravallo walked between us with the same peculiar theatrical swagger. We passed nobody—a fact which pleased me a great deal—and the evening was now sufficiently dark for me to cease worrying about Auntie getting a lucky glimpse of the procession.

Guelvada began to sing softly under his breath in Flemish. He seemed happy. Maybe he was looking forward to having a good time with Ravallo.

We came to the cottage, made our way to the back door, went inside. I switched on my torch, shielding the light with my fingers, and pushed Ravallo before me into the small room with the high window.

I told Guelvada to black out the window. He did this by the simple expedient of taking off Ravallo's coat and hanging it over the window frame. I took my fingers off the torch bulb.

Ravallo stood, in his shirtsleeves, in the centre of the empty room. He had the same bored expression on his face, but there was a flicker of something else in his eyes.

I put my left hand in my jacket pocket and brought

out a length of strong fishing twine. I handed it to Guelvada.

"Tie him up," I said.

Guelvada took the twine, stepped towards Ravallo.

Ravallo shrugged his shoulders again—this time the gesture was more marked. There was an air of hopelessness about his attitude. He said :

"What do you expect me to say ? What information do you expect to get from me ? I know nothing. Why should I ? I am not sufficiently important to be told things—to know things."

Nobody said anything. He put his hands over his face, wearily dropped them ; stood looking at Guelvada, who faced him with the same quiet smile on his face.

Ernie was definitely enjoying himself.

"Tie him up," I said. "And use his handkerchief for a gag—if we *have* to have a gag. I don't want a lot of noise. And search him."

The Belgian grinned. He said : "But of course." He got busy on Ravallo. He tied his wrists and ankles expertly.

I put my gun in my pocket. I took a quick look through the other rooms in the cottage. I found a wooden box in the rear room. I brought it back and put it in the centre of the floor.

I stood, looking at Ravallo. I could feel Ernie Guelvada watching me out of the corner of his eye. He was wondering just how far I was going; whether I was going right through with the job, and putting Ravallo through it to get the information I wanted, or whether I was merely bluffing.

I wasn't bluffing. I'd made up my mind about that. I've seen too much of what Germans and Japanese have done to people to worry about hurting an agent in order to get information I wanted. I knew just what he'd be doing to me if I was in his place.

I was wondering just how much Ravallo knew ; just how important he was in the scheme of things. I believed he was *very* important. As I'd told Guelvada it was certain that he must have met Sammy, some time or other, in order to have imitated his voice. Now another thing occurred to me. *Somebody* had imitated *my* voice ; that somebody who had telephoned to Alison Fredericks at the Vaile flat and told her to go to Namur Street. She wouldn't have gone unless she'd been certain it was me. If she hadn't been certain she would have telephoned me first. And she hadn't. She hadn't because she believed she'd been talking to me. Instead of which she'd been talking to Ravallo.

If this was so then Ravallo had heard *me* talking some time. Where ? And the only place I could think of would be the party at the Marinettes. That's where he could have heard me talking.

He was probably one of the two men who had gone round to Sammy's room after he'd drunk the Mickey Finn and done a little searching there. That meant that he was working with Auntie—a fact that was corroborated by her presence here, in Walling. Probably she was his particular " contact."

And he was in a hell of a good spot to work. He was a vaudeville *artiste*, a travelling showman, playing cinemas and small music halls all over the country. His presence at any particular place would not be suspect, because of his job.

This gave me an idea. It was all the tea in China to a bad egg that neither Auntie nor anyone else suspected my presence in Walling. It was pure chance and our luck that I had seen her. Therefore, it was just possible that Ravello would havs been a little more careless than usual. Because he had not—for the last few days—been doing anything more dangerous than imitating Sammy's voice on the telephone, he would be taking things easy. This might be good for me.

I began to think about Freeby. I wondered what Freeby was at ; whether he had tried to get in touch with me ; whether our little friend Bettina Vaile had tried to pull any fast ones. My idea was that she would lead Freeby off somewhere well off the beaten track, hoping that I would go after her, allowing the job, whatever it was, to be done and done quickly.

I said : " Sit down on the box, Ravallo."

Ravallo hopped over to the box and seated himself. He

seemed a most docile prisoner. I imagined that he was merely playing for time, hoping for a break of some sort.

Ernie Guelvada stood by the side of the dirty fireplace, leaning on the dilapidated mantelpiece. He was smoking quietly. His eyes never left the face of the man seated on the box.

I lit a cigarette. I stood leaning against the wall, looking at Ravallo. I said :

" Listen . . . and make it as easy as you can for yourself. You're working for one of the Himmler External organisations. You're associated with a rather trim good-looking woman with very blue eyes. She went to your dressing-room at the cinema to see you to-night. I want to know what for. That's the first thing.

" The second thing is this : Yesterday, or possibly the day before, probably on the instructions of that woman, you telephoned to a Miss Carew at Chippinsfield. You imitated the voice of her nephew—Sammy Carew—which you had heard and which you had studied carefully. You told her that you were her nephew ; that you expected a young woman named Janine to call and make enquiries about you or how she could get in touch with you. You told Miss Carew that on no account was she to let Janine know that you had telephoned. You gave her instructions as to what she should tell Janine when she came. You warned her especially that if I came about the place—and you gave her a description of me—she was to tell me nothing. No matter what I might say.

" I want to know exactly what you told her. Next— I want to know about a lady called Mrs. Vaile. You may or may not know about her. If you *do* know anything spill it. It will save you a lot of trouble.

" In fact I want to know the whole book—everything. I'm going to get it out of you one way or another. When you've talked we shall check up on what you say. We shall leave you here and come back for you when we have checked up. If you've lied or tried any funny business we shall start work on you again. You understand ? "

Ravallo smiled a little. He said in a soft voice : " I understand very well."

I said to Guelvada : " Talk to him, Ernie. . . ."

Guelvada came forward. He stood in front of Ravallo, a little to one side of him looking at him with his head on one side, smiling—most unpleasantly.

He said : " My friend, The Great Ravallo, you listen to me. I am Guelvada. Maybe you have heard of me. I am a specialist in making people talk. Always they talk for Ernie Guelvada—in the long run . . . hey ? Listen . . . why don't you save yourself a helluva lot of grief and talk without some more trouble ? "

Ravallo said nothing.

Guelvada went on : " I think you are a very obstinate goddam type. That's O.K. with me. I've got something special for you. I tell you what I've got for you. First of all I'm going to give you a little Japanese stuff just to show you what's what. If you decide that you want to talk any time just wag your head from side to side. You got that ? O.K. After that, if you don't talk, I'm going to give you the water. You know about the water ? I bet you do. Mr. Himmler is very fond of the water business. He used to use it in Columbia House in Berlin on the Jews. It isn't very pleasant. Not on your goddam life . . . hey ? "

I said : " You know, Ravallo, you ought to know about Guelvada. He's a very nasty fellow. Perhaps you'd like to hear why ? "

He smiled again. The same non-committal smile. He shrugged his shoulders slightly as much as to say : " Well . . . if it amuses you . . ."

I went on : " Guelvada here was engaged to a young woman—a Belgian. Well . . . when the Germans came along to her village they weren't very nice to her. In fact they were very unpleasant. Eventually she died. I think she must have been rather glad to die. . . . Naturally all this didn't please Guelvada very much. It's had a peculiar effect on him. It's made Germans—people like you—very unpopular with him. He likes getting his own back. If I leave you to him you're going to have a very nasty time. Well . . . are you going to talk ? "

Ravallo looked at me ; then he looked at Guelvada. He grinned contemptuously. He said, in German : " To hell with you both."

Guelvada took a step forward and put his forefinger on

Ravallo's shoulder. He put his finger on the shoulder nerve and then, with the other hand, put on the Japanese neck lock.

Ravallo began to squirm. His face was ashen. In a minute beads of sweat stood out on his forehead.

Guelvada took his hands away, stepped back. He stood, his head on one side, looking at Ravallo.

He spread his hands. He turned to me. He said : " The boy's tough. They get like that, you know. Well . . . I shall give him the water. *Nobody* can stand that. Is there a bucket or a tin here . . . hey ? "

I said : " There's an old water bucket in the yard outside, then there's a tap in the kitchen."

He nodded. " And I can use the twine to swing it," he said. " That's O.K. Well . . . he goddam wants it and he's going to get it."

He went outside.

I said to Ravallo : " Guelvada's going to give you the water torture. You know what that is, don't you ? He's going to swing a bucket of water over your head with a tiny hole stuck in the bottom of the bucket. The water begins to drip on your head. Not regularly. He arranges that by swinging the bucket slightly. No one has ever been known to stand that continuous and irregular drip-drip on the head for very long. You'll *have* to talk. Why not now ? "

Ravallo looked at me. His eyes were tired. He looked almost bored. He said : " To hell with you and your accursed country."

I shrugged my shoulders. I said : " Well . . . you've had your chance."

Guelvada came back with the bucket. He put it down on the floor and lit a cigarette. He was looking at Ravallo.

I said : " Get on with it, Ernie. He's *got* to talk. In the meantime I've got an idea. I'll try it. Listen to what he has to say when he decides that it's healthier for him to tell the story. I'll be back as soon as I can."

Guelvada said : " That's O.K. with me. I shall deal with him systematically. Rely on Guelvada. The boyo will talk all right."

He began to take off his coat.

I went out of the cottage and began to walk down the road towards the lane that led to the stage door of the cinema. It was quite dark now and a lovely night. There was a soft breeze and I began to wonder what life would be like *if* there wasn't a war on, *if* one could do what one liked with life. I took five minutes' mental rest thinking like that.

Then I came back to the matter in hand. I began to think about Janine. Supposing they were wise to Janine—and I had come to the regretful conclusion that they were. They would imagine that she had some sort of working contract either with Sammy or with me. They had seen Sammy with her, and they had known of my desire to get in touch with her. Their one idea would be to make her talk—probably in very much the same way as we were making Ravallo talk. They'd want to know about Sammy and they'd want to know about me. And the fact that she knew little of Sammy's game and none at all of mine wouldn't help her one little bit.

Unwittingly Janine had played into their hands. She'd left the picture post-card of The Old Moor Lodge in her room, and worse than that she'd probably left the A.B.C. Railway timetable open at Chippinsfield. They'd guessed that she was going down to talk to Sammy's aunt and they'd got in first. Ravallo had been put in to telephone Miss Carew; to say that he was Sammy and that he expected that Janine would be down; that she was to be told so-and-so and to go to so-and-so, but that his name was not to be mentioned.

It was a chance and it had come off. Janine had been told to go somewhere and she'd probably gone and walked into something not so good.

Which was the reason why I was prepared to be very tough with Ravallo.

By now I had entered the lane that ran down to the stage door passage. I walked quietly in the shadow of the wall until I came to the stage door. This was set a few feet back in the wall, and I was able to stand in the opening out of sight and relax.

I could hear nothing. By now, I hoped, the cinema would be deserted. I thought it unlikely that, in these days, any cleaning would be done at night.

After a few more minutes I started work on the door. It was a double door with an old-fashioned lock and I had it open in five minutes. I stepped inside, closed the doors behind me, locked them and stood in the stone passage—listening.

The place was as quiet as a churchyard. I thanked my lucky stars for the black-out regulations, switched on my electric torch, looked about me. I was standing in a stone passage that ran, from the back of the cinema, to the stage. A few yards down the passage, on each side, were flights of stone steps curving round to the smaller passages above in which were situated the dressing and other rooms.

I went up the stairway on the right. The first room in the passage was evidently used as a musical store room. In it were Panatrope records and recording material. The next door was the manager's office, and the third and last room was the staff room.

I went back to the main passage and tried the stairway on the left. Affixed to the first door along the passage above was a card—*The Great Ravallo*—*The World's Greatest Mimic*. The door was locked, but it took me only two minutes to deal with that. I stepped into the room, found the light switch, switched on the light, closed the door and stood with my back to it looking about me.

The room was the usual sort of vaudeville *artistes'* dressing-room. There were a few photographs of Ravallo stuck in the mirror over the make-up table and some publicity cut from local newspapers. An evening suit and accessories hung on a coat hanger, draped with a dust cloth, and, in the corner, stood the usual wicker theatrical travelling basket.

I began to search. I went over the place thoroughly. I even investigated the linings of the coats and waistcoats, the heels of shoes—everything. I forced the lock of the travelling basket, spread the contents on the floor and systematically went through everything.

I found nothing. I tidied up ; put everything back

where it had come from. Then I went over and sat down on the stool before the make-up table.

There were the usual sticks of make-up on the table, and the powder and grease towels and accessories, a box of cigarettes and half a bottle of whisky. There was also a book—a small leather book. I opened it. It was Ravallo's date book.

I examined it carefully. It was the usual vaudeville *artistes'* date book and it gave the dates that The Great Ravallo had played for the last three months. Most of them were small provincial and country cinemas that ran two or three turns on the bill. Here and there was a date at one of the smaller Music Halls in the provinces.

I flipped over the page that had the Walling Cinema entry. There was a blank space for the next day—Sunday—and I turned the page over with a peculiar feeling of expectancy. The page showed the entry "The Weathervane Club," Pellsberry, and noted the fact that Ravallo was to do two shows per evening.

I turned to the next page. It was blank. The date at The Weathervane Club was The Great Ravallo's last date.

Which was what I had expected and which, having regard to the position, was just as well !

I put the book back on the table ; looked carefully round the dressing-room, arranged everything, more or less, as it had been on my entrance, switched off the light and went out.

I locked the door, went downstairs to the stage entrance, slipped outside quietly and locked the doors after me.

I began to walk down the passageway. I wondered if Ravallo had decided to talk. Then I decided that it was pretty certain that he would talk and that the only question was how much.

But he might be clever. He might do what espionage agents—on both sides—have done when faced with a difficult situation. He might tell enough truth to make it apparent that it *was* true but not enough for us to do anything about. And it was going to be difficult for us to check.

The night had become suddenly dark and a few spots of rain began to fall. I stepped out quickly, along the dirt road that led to our cottage. I considered, cynically, just what the respectable and well-disposed inhabitants of Walling would have to say if they knew that an empty cottage in their salubrious district was, at the moment, being used as a make-shift torture chamber. I shrugged my shoulders at that. Some very odd but necessary things have happened in this war that would never see the light of day.

I turned across the field and approached the cottage from the back. By this time, I thought, Ernie Guelvada would be sitting down on *some* information or our friend Ravallo would possibly not be feeling so well.

Walking across the damp field I began to think about Sammy; to wonder what actually had happened on the night of the party; to wonder what it was that Sammy had that our friends were so interested in. Possibly a document or a photograph or both. I wondered what Sammy, faced with the situation that had confronted him on the night of the Marinette party, had decided to do. Quite obviously something had happened at that party which had decided him to lie low, not to recognise me, not to talk to me, not to do anything that would give any move in the game away. Why?

The answer to that one was that Sammy knew or guessed that he was on the top line; that he was dealing with a damned dangerous crowd who weren't going to stick at anything.

It had seemed the safest thing to do was to get cockeyed, and he had come to that conclusion *at the party*— and not before. If he'd discovered something *before* the party he could have got into touch with the Old Man and had the information passed on to me. But he hadn't. Another thing was that Janine had been at the party with him. Probably Sammy had taken her to the party as a sort of blind or red herring, calculated to give the impression to anyone particularly interested that he was merely having an evening out with a girl friend.

He had carried this impression on by seeing Janine home afterwards. But he had said nothing to her of his suspicions. He had said nothing to her about me. Why? The answer to the one might easily be that Sammy believed that the less that Janine knew at that moment might be the better *for her*. He also believed that with luck there would be a chance of getting in touch with me fairly soon. Probably he had intended to do that the next morning.

But if he *had* had something that they wanted—something important—what would he do with it ? He had said in his letter he had come out of the stupor produced by the doctored drink they had prepared for him to find a couple of men in his room. That meant that somebody —probably my blue-eyed friend Auntie—had doctored the drink whilst he was at the party, and that such search as they had had time to make up to then had revealed nothing.

So they'd knocked off Sammy and they'd probably tried out all sorts of things on him first to make him talk. And they'd failed. I couldn't imagine anybody making Sammy talk—not by any means whatsoever—if he didn't *want* to talk.

Which meant that the thing—the document or the photograph or whatever it was—that they were so keen to get their hands on was still unfound. That it was still where Sammy had hidden it. And it was not hidden on him otherwise they'd have got it, and it was not in his room because they'd searched there, and it was sufficiently important for Sammy to want to have around where he could get at it quickly when he wanted it. Which meant that it was going to be *operationally* important to us on the job we had in hand. The job that he was, in all probability, going to tell me all about the day after the Marinette party.

Just how much or how little Janine knew was also an unknown quantity at the moment. But she knew *something*. She knew enough to want to keep out of Auntie's way when that good lady had gone to see her at Verity Street ; she had known enough to evade Auntie and take a chance on slipping round to Kinnoul Street to have a look round, to search for *something*. She must have known, or guessed, what that something was.

Possibly it was through Janine that Sammy had collected the item. I realised that five minutes' talk with that beautiful lady might save me a great deal of trouble. Well . . . the thing to do was to find her. Maybe Ravallo knew where she was.

If Sammy and I had been able to have a talk. *If* . . . As it was the job had started so badly, been so gummed up by his death, that Janine instead of being a help had been almost a liability.

I wondered where she was ? What they had on ice for her. I thought that it wasn't going to be so good for Janine. I imagined the sort of treatment she'd get from " Mrs. Bettina Vaile " or Auntie. Both of these ladies belonged to the type that delighted in pulling butterflies' wings off.

Sammy had said nothing of me to Janine. Obviously. She had known nothing of me, and quite rightly she had distrusted me. Also she would continue to do so until such time as I could disclose to her facts which would establish me as being on the right side.

But he *had* said one thing to Janine. He had told her about his aunt—Miss Carew—at Chippenfield. It was probably Sammy who had given her that picture postcard of The Old Moor Lodge. And the gesture would be characteristic of Sammy.

He would have told her, in all probability, that if she got into any sort of jam she might go down there and see Miss Carew. And for reasons best known to himself this was all he proposed to say to her. Why ?

I could guess the answer to that one. It was because, at the party, Sammy had come to the conclusion that they were on to him and *on to me*. So he kept away from me. His only contact with me, and that was instantaneous and obviously unnoticed by anyone, was when he had slipped the piece of paper with his address on it into my pocket. The idea was that if anything happened to him that night—*and he had an idea that it might*—I should have something to work from—even if it was only his address.

Only his address ! Something clicked in my mind. I stopped walking and stood still in the now damp field, twenty-five yards from the back door of the cottage, pondering on the implication of these words. Possibly I was on to something—at last.

I remembered that odd fact about the Kinnoul Street house—Auntie's house. And that was that the front door seemed always to be on the latch ; that anyone could come in or go out. Well . . . there are lots of apartments houses in London where the front entrance is open so that people may go in and out.

So all sorts and conditions of people could easily get into the house—if they had business there. And Sammy had known this. He had known that it was not always necessary to ring the bell and wait for the door to be answered. He had in fact known that it would be quite easy for me, if anything happened to him, *to get into the house*.

Well . . . I could easily deal with that situation. I began to move once more in the direction of the cottage door and I began to think of The Great Ravallo. I concluded that he would not be feeling quite so great. I wondered just what state Guelvada's water treatment had reduced him.

I pushed open the door and went in. I stood, in the narrow dark passage, pushed the door to behind me and listened. I could hear nothing at all. I switched on my electric torch, dimming the light with my fingers, walked along the passage, looked into the kitchen, saw nothing ; continued for a few steps further and turned into the room where I had left Guelvada and Ravallo.

I stood in the doorway looking upon a most peculiar scene. Seated on the box by the side of the fireplace, was Guelvada. The light from a piece of candle perched precariously on the edge of the mantelpiece fell on his face. His head was supported by one hand. He presented a picture of the most abject dejection. An unlit half-smoked cigarette stub hung from the corner of his mouth. He gazed dismally at the floor, and when I came in raised his eyes to me with an almost piteous expression of complete and utter helplessness.

Obviously Ernie wasn't so pleased with life.

Against the wall, on the side opposite to the door, Ravallo's body was laid out. Quite obviously he was dead. His face was composed and he lay, stretched in a more or less natural attitude, against the wood panelling.

I said : " Well . . . ? "

Guelvada shrugged his shoulders. He took the cigarette end out of his mouth and threw it into the fireplace with an almost venomous energy. Then he jerked his thumb in the direction of the departed Ravallo.

He said : " He's dead. Goddam it, very and quite dead. I am infuriated. I, Guelvada, have been made a fool of. I am steamed up plenty . . . hey? What the hell . . . ! "

I shrugged my shoulders. " And he didn't say anything ? " I asked.

" He did not have a chance to say anything," said Guelvada. " Immediately after you had gone I got the bucket and started to rig up the apparatus for the water. When I was going out of the room I said to him : ' My friend, in a little while you will be *glad* to talk to Ernest Guelvada. You will be glad to stop the terrible drip-drip-drip of the water on your head. I shall not have to *ask* you to talk. You will love talking. Do you understand, my friend ? '

" That is what I said to him. He looked at me with those funny eyes of his and he told me to go to hell. He told me to go to hell in a very soft voice that should have made me suspicious then. Then he called me by a very rude name. Then I went out of the room.

" When I came back he was dead. He had fallen off the box and was lying on the floor."

I said : " Poison, I suppose ? "

" Right," said Guelvada. " He must have taken it when he put his face in his hands, when he pretended to be distressed. You remember? Just before I tied him up. Goddam it, he must have been laughing at us inside of him. The louse ! "

He began to swear. He used some of the most terrible language I have ever heard in my life about the family, relations and descendants—if any—of the unfortunate Ravallo. I think he went on for about four minutes without repeating an adjective. He was really *very* angry.

I lit a cigarette and let him finish. I said : " Listen, Guelvada ; just forget your annoyance for a few minutes and concentrate on what I'm saying."

I pointed to Ravallo's body. "That was our last chance of getting next to something that mattered, really quickly," I said. "Well, now we've got to get busy. We've got to try and find this Janine person. And we've *got* to get a move on. Or else——"

Guelvada nodded. "Precisely," he said. "If we don't find her and they get her they'll *make* her talk. They won't be at all nice to her, those —— I know them."

"It's not a matter of *if* they get her," I said. "It's all the tea in China that they've got her now. This fellow Ravallo gave Miss Carew some instructions to give her. Well, you can imagine what they were. Probably she was told to go to some place or other and they were waiting for her when she got there. And if she *does* know anything they'll get it all right. They've probably started work on her already."

Guelvada said : "What shall we do? Where do we go from here . . . hey? Or do we go anywhere?"

"I'm going back to town," I said. "I'm going to see if Freeby's got anything. Something may have broken at that end."

"I should like to come too," said Guelvada. "Very goddam much. I am now very interested in this business. Also I have not yet had an opportunity of killing somebody. Maybe I'll get a break sometime . . . hey?"

"Maybe," I said. "But you're not coming to London. Directly I've gone get rid of that body somehow. It's quite dark now and you can get it hidden somewhere around here. Then go back to The Crown and take a room. To-morrow, keep an eye on the stage door of the cinema."

"For what?" he asked.

"For Auntie," I said. "Use your brains. She's not going to hear anything from Ravallo. She's down here in Walling and she's not here for her health. She and he were working together. To-day's Thursday and he has the week to finish here. I've got his next date. I know where he was going. But it's certain that Auntie will want to get in touch with him before then. She could always meet him in his dressing-room and they could talk as much as they like unobserved. So she'll go there again.

If she does you've got to stick to her like a kitten to a hot brick, Ernie. You've got to find where she goes when she leaves Walling. Incidentally there's one good thing about Ravallo being dead."

" Is there ? " he asked. " Well . . . if there is, I don't see it. What is the good thing, Mr. Kells ? "

" She's going to wonder what the devil has happened to Ravallo," I said. " When he doesn't turn up for his performance at the cinema to-morrow the news is going to get round the town and she's going to hear it. She'll skedaddle round there like a fire engine to find out what she can. Then she's going to get windy. She'll believe that we were on to Ravallo and that we've knocked him off. *And she'll do something or go somewhere.* She'll have to take some sort of action. Your business is to find out what. You understand ? "

" I understand," he said. " Of course you are absolutely and entirely right, Mr. Kells. You're telling me." He looked at the body. " But I would have liked to have put half an hour in on that so-and-so. Ah well . . ." He gave a resigned shrug of the shoulders.

" You'll get a chance of killing somebody yet—if they don't get you first," I said. " Well . . . good-night . . . clear up the mess here and get on to Auntie as soon as you can."

I gave him a detailed description of that charming lady.

" Where do I get in touch with you ? " he asked.

" Ring my apartment in London," I said. " If I'm not there I'll leave somebody to take messages. Good-night."

I went out. It was raining hard and the night was very dark. That was one good thing anyhow. I turned up the collar of my coat and began to walk back to Walling.

The luck hadn't been so good.

It was well past midnight when I arrived back in London. I went straight to my apartment, left the car outside, found the hall porter. Apparently nobody had asked for me or tried to get in touch with me or telephoned or done anything at all. In fact everything had been so quiet and well-behaved that I began to feel slightly annoyed with one and all.

I took a hot and cold shower, put on fresh clothes and gave myself a large drink. I needed it. I was feeling that I was going around in circles and not getting anywhere at all ; that in a minute I should believe I'd dreamed it all.

I put my feet up on the mantelpiece and began to think about Sammy. Right from the start in this business Sammy had appeared *not* to run true to form—a business which of itself was very unlike Sammy, who was a person who always *did* run true to form. Sammy might do something that was vague or that *appeared* odd or ambiguous or incongruous or just damn stupid but he always had an idea in his head and he always left something sticking out to show you what was in his mind. Until this job.

And if anyone could show me anything sticking out or plain to the eye I felt I'd give them a medal. Personally, I was beginning to feel near beat.

In my business you do a lot of things without a great deal of reason. You must. Most of the time you're guessing, and success or failure is just the number of times that you guess right. It was of course obvious to me that Sammy had expected to contact me and talk to me either on the night of the party or the next day. He must have. Something had happened on the night of the party to make him change his mind.

And I could make a guess about that one. Or could I ? I wondered just how right—or wrong—I'd be if I came to the conclusion that the reason why he had decided not to talk to me at all—not to write me a line *before* he went to the party—or to write a line to the Old Man to pass on to me—was because he was uncertain about something. Quite apart from any conclusions that he'd come to *at the party*—conclusions that had decided him to make a night of it, cut out business and get cockeyed—Sammy had been uncertain about something *before* the party. Otherwise he'd have done something about me. I thought that this made some sort of sense.

I gave myself another shot of Vat 69 ; put my feet

back on the mantelpiece, slumped back in the armchair and gave myself up to a deep consideration of the lady we knew as Janine.

That one was very smart and very clever and very beautiful. She had the makings, lots of allure and quite an issue of brains—if I knew anything about women. Her behaviour—so far as I was concerned—had been very odd and funny from the start. Right from the beginning I had considered her to be on the other side playing some sort of game with blue-eyed Auntie, the white-faced boyo and Mrs. Bettina Vaile. That had been my first idea. I'd thrown it overboard when I'd received the letter from Sammy. And that was the only reason I had for throwing it overboard. But it might be very funny if my first idea about her had been right.

If this was so then Sammy had to be wrong and that was not like Sammy. But why shouldn't he be wrong? Everybody can slip up once, and when you're dealing with a woman like the Janine piece, and you have a temperament like Sammy, well . . .

Who the hell was Janine anyway? Nobody except Sammy had ever heard of her, met her, or, apparently, seen her. The Old Man certainly hadn't. Otherwise he'd have told me.

You've got to realise that the last time I'd seen Sammy was in the Pas de Calais. We'd agreed to separate. He was to go first and I was to follow when it seemed safe. The idea being that they shouldn't get us both.

But it was a stone certainty that we'd been missed immediately. And if the German " I " people had got on to us—and there was every reason to believe that they would—they would have us taped by the duplicate photographs on our identity cards and would send out S.O.S.s before you could light a cigarette.

It was quite possible that by the time Sammy arrived in England, the Mrs. Vaile-Auntie *clique* had been tipped off that we were trying to get back home, and were looking for us before we'd even got here.

And it was some time between the time that he'd left me and the time he'd arrived here and talked to the Old Man that Sammy had discovered whatever it was he had discovered. And it was quite on the cards that this—briefly that there was a Himmler External Section working over here on the Flying Bomb thing—had been divulged to him by Janine.

And why not? Sammy had met her some time between the time he had left me and the night of the party. That was one fact I was certain about anyway. Very well, it might be that Janine had told him about the German section; that the original information had come from her.

And this would make Sammy believe that she was on the up and up. He would believe her. He would take the fact that she had told him this (supported as it must have been by other information about herself) as a guarantee of her integrity. And he would act on her information.

And where had it got him?

A very funny idea came into my head. One I didn't like a bit. Supposing, for the sake of argument, that Janine was working for the enemy. Supposing she was one of the people who had been told that two men—originally believed to be German Artillery officers, attached to the Rocket Batteries—were in fact British agents; that they were probably on their way back to England. Supposing she had been given a detailed description of these two men? Well, she started off by knowing us. That was one to her. Then somehow she'd picked up Sammy—she might even have been put in to pick him up *before* he left France—and then supposing she'd told him the story of the Himmler Section working in London. She knew (a) that Sammy would believe it because we both knew that the thing that had been worrying the German Rocket people on the French and Belgian coasts was that they could get no directional information about where the Flying Bombs were dropping, and (b) that he would probably be put on the job of running the Himmler Section down.

In other words, they would be fore-armed against us; they would know who we were; and with Janine pretending to be on our side they would be in a nice position to play funny games with us. This, added to the fact that I knew they were playing for a climax; that they were getting a little desperate; that they had to do something and damned quickly, would make a very good argument if you wanted to argue like that.

Accepting this theory, then it might easily have been that Sammy—who was no fool—had come to the time of the night of the party believing that Janine was playing ball with him. Well . . . supposing that sometime on that day, some time before the party, a doubt had crept into his mind ? Then what would he do ?

Surely, exactly what he had done.

His first thought would be for the job. His second to protect me so that if they got him I could go on with it. So he laid off me. He wrote me no note, cut out telephoning, gave me the only tip-off that he could at the party by getting cockeyed. Slipping me the one essential bit of information—his address ; saying nothing to me of Janine and nothing to her of me.

That is what he would do.

After which, before he was killed, he took the trouble to tell me, in his note, that Janine was for us, that she was on our side. Well . . . what about that one ?

But there could be a come-back to that one. *That might not have been the truth. Supposing Sammy had inserted the bit about Janine in the letter to ensure its delivery to me !* Here he was throwing an envelope out of a window hoping that somebody would put it in a post-box or deliver it. He knew damned well that it might easily have fallen into their hands. It had to be lying in the road somewhere outside the place where he was prisoner. Supposing Sammy—still as clever as ever—had worked out that in order to get me sucked in as well as himself *they would allow the letter to be delivered.* And why not ? The rest of the information in it was worth Sweet Fanny Adams . . . nothing at all for all practical purposes.

I finished my drink and concluded that doubt was a very nasty thing.

Janine's attitude from the start allowed for her being on either side. Theirs or ours. You could work it out which way you liked and set it to music. You could play it either way and where would it get you ?

Even her visit to Miss Carew could be for one of two reasons. One to find out who Sammy was working for to give him such information or such documents as she had—if she had any—or to discover *for them* who was the top man in the British *anti* Section working against them.

I came to the conclusion that life could be tough. Very tough.

After which I got my hat and went out. I felt that Verity Street was calling.

I stopped the car at the Mulbery Street end of Verity Street, parked it in a patch of shadow ; began to walk down the street on the side opposite Janine's place.

The rain had stopped, the wind had dropped and a moon had come out. The night wasn't bad and the heaviness and heat which I had previously associated with this neighbourhood was conspicuous by its absence. I decided to take this for an omen, although I must say I am not the sort of person who wastes a lot of time playing about with omens.

As I approached the house I could see a sliver of light coming from under the blackout curtain from Janine's sitting-room. I stopped and lit a cigarette. I thought the time had come when that lady and I should do a spot more talking together.

I crossed the road and pressed the bell button over the card " Janine " which still showed in its little metal frame. Nothing happened. I pressed the bell again and kept my finger on it. Nobody bothered. Then I knocked on the door.

A minute or so passed and the door opened. Inside the dimly lit hallway was the landlady. She looked at me with a certain subdued hostility in her eyes. I had the idea that she didn't like me a lot. I wondered why.

I said : " Good-evening. How do you do ? Is Miss Janine at home ? "

" It's very late," she said acidly. " We don't usually have callers at this time."

I said : " I'm sorry about that. By the way, I suppose you remember me. I'm the Police Officer who called here yesterday."

She said : " Yes ? " Her tone was a trifle insolent. " You don't look like a police officer to me."

" What do I look like ? " I asked her. " A performing seal ? Anyhow, perhaps you'll be good enough to answer my question. I want to see Miss Janine."

She said : " You can't see her. She isn't here."

I nodded. " Has she been here since I was here last time ? " I asked.

She shook her head. " She hasn't come back yet," she said.

I lit a fresh cigarette. " Who's in her sitting-room at the moment ? " I asked. " Even if you don't think I look like a Police Officer you'll remember I paid the rent. You haven't let those rooms to any one else . . . have you ? "

She said : " No, I haven't. The rooms are being cleaned. We've been busy and haven't had time to do it before."

I yawned. " Too bad," I said. " Never mind . . . better luck next time. If and when you see Miss Janine you might tell her that I've called and that we might meet some time . . . even if it's not to be here . . . say round at Kinnoul Street. That might be more convenient for her." I grinned at her.

She said acidly : " Very well." She closed the door with a bang.

I began to walk back towards the car. It was fairly obvious that somebody—probably Janine—had been putting in some heavy work on the landlady. I began to think that perhaps I didn't like Janine so very much ; that some of my ideas of earlier in the evening might have been so true that you'd be surprised.

I started up the car and began to drive down Verity Street. As I passed the house I could see that the sliver of light no longer showed from Janine's sitting-room. Somebody had seen to that.

I turned off and began to drive in the direction of Kinnoul Street. I thought I might as well make a round of calls now that I was on the job. I thought it would be amusing if I rang the bell at the Kinnoul Street house and Auntie opened it. But I didn't think so. I had an idea that Auntie had not been back there since the night of the pepper-pot incident and probably never would go back. That house would be just another memory to her.

I stopped the car down the street in a Mews, switched off the lights and finished the journey on foot. The house was in complete darkness. It had the air of a house that was empty and dusty. There was something about the place I didn't like.

I rang the bell and nobody took any notice. Then I tried the front dor. It was locked this time. Then I noticed, stuck on the ground floor window, the large black " E " of the Civil Defence.

The street was quiet ; the moon had gone behind a cloud. I took out my bunch of keys and started work on the door. It was quite easy. I was inside inside three minutes.

I closed the door behind me and stood in the passage-way. I knew the geography of the house pretty well. On the right of the passage was the dining-room where I had my last interview with Auntie. Upstairs was Sammy's old bedroom and above that Auntie's room.

I went into the dining-room and switched on my torch. The place was as I had seen it last time. Auntie's supper things were still on the table, the furniture in the same positions, and Auntie's chair still overturned on the floor as it had fallen when she made her hurried exit.

Apparently nobody had been back there since my last visit. But somebody had telephoned to the Civil Defence people that the house was empty. And that was that.

I went upstairs to Sammy's room. It was just the same as I had seen it last time. His clothes were still folded into a neat pile on the bed. The blackout was down and I switched on the electric light and stood leaning on the bed rail, thinking about Sammy.

I lit a cigarette. I didn't suppose that Sammy had been very surprised when he came out of that Mickey Finn and found the two boyos searching his room. Nothing ever surprised Sammy. But he must have thought it odd that they should think he'd been damned fool enough to hide whatever they were looking for in his own bedroom.

But the joke was that nobody ever did what anybody

thought they were going to do—except sometimes when they did because they thought the other people would think it so very obvious that it was even worth while trying to get away with it. A little involved perhaps, but understandable in a racket like ours. It was often worth while working out what people would think one would do and then double-crossing oneself. Sammy was a person who thought rather along those lines.

I went out of the bedroom and up the stairs. I thought it damned funny that I should be walking about a house that had been the scene of at least two dramas—if you can call my affair with the pepper-pot a drama—that was empty of people but full of furniture and knick-knacks and atmosphere and what-will-you.

I pushed open the door on the floor above and went into Auntie's bedroom. I flashed my torch about the place, saw that the blackout curtain were pulled, found the electric light switch, turned on the light. Everything about the room was normal. I looked at the bed—and believe me I would have been surprised if Auntie had been in it wearing a night cap—and saw that it was made, with the bedspread turned down, just as if someone was about to get into it.

The room was attractive. The bed was against the wall on the left of the doorway. The room was large, carpeted all over, and over against the bay window, on the right of the door, was a large and rather handsome desk. The blotter and ink-wells and pens were set out on the desk, with a desk diary, pen wiper, and all the other bits and pieces that old ladies like around the places they write letters. There was a stationery rack, and a tray of nibs and paper clips and even a book of stamps. I gathered that Auntie was a rather meticulous piece when she wasn't cutting someone's throat or pulling some other mayhem of a like nature.

And on the mantelpiece, over the fireplace, which was a gas job filled with imitation coal, was her photograph in a silver frame, the one I'd noticed on my previous visit. I went over and looked at it.

Photographs, as you probably know, are odd things. The camera often sees a lot of things that the human eye misses, and whoever had taken the picture of Auntie was no mean photographer. It was a full-face picture, and it looked at me out of its silver frame with an expression that said as clearly as any words—" Nuts to you ! "

Auntie's expression was just like that.

I picked up the frame and stood looking at it. Then I took it under the electric light and took another closer look at it. I was definitely interested in the facial characteristics of this rather nasty woman. I took a really good look and decided to put it back on the mantelpiece.

Then one of those things happened. One of those things that happen once or twice in a lifetime. The back of the picture frame, which was of the usual black cardboard sort, held in place by a couple of small hasps, fell off. Auntie's picture fell out of the frame on to the floor. I was left holding the silver frame and the glass, and when I bent down to pick up the pieces, I saw, under the picture-back, a small brown envelope.

It was about four inches square and I knew exactly what it was. When I saw it my heart began to pound. I dropped the rest of the stuff on the floor ; picked it up and opened it. Inside were three three-inch square films. I knew exactly what they were. They were the usual " I " process for pictures of plans or documents needing reduction used by all our anti-espionage or H.Q. " I " services.

The stuff was reduced too small for me to see what it was. But I wasn't bothering what it was. I *knew* what it was. I knew that it was the stuff that Sammy had hidden behind Auntie's picture because he knew goddam well that that was the one place they wouldn't look for it—*in her room.*

For the first time in this business I began to feel a little excited. I took a piece of writing paper from Auntie's desk and tore it into pieces to fit the envelope so that it still appeared to have the films inside. Then I restuck the envelope neatly ; put it back in its place in the picture frame and replaced the frame on the mantelpiece. I went over to the writing desk, took one of Auntie's envelopes, addressed it to the Old Man, grabbed a piece of notepaper, wrote on it : " *Urgent. Please enlarge immediately,*" put the films and the note in the envelope, stuck it down, put one of Auntie's stamps on it and made for the door.

I went down the stairs with the Mauser in my hand feeling not so bad, and with the definite idea in my head that if anybody got in the way they were going to get it where it would hurt most. I left the door on the latch.

At the end of Kinnoul Street, on the corner, was a post-box. I posted my letter, lit a cigarette and went back to Auntie's.

I went up the stairs to her bedroom and relaxed. I felt almost happy. I was wise to Sammy.

Sammy had been on the top line and he'd played it the only way he could. Somehow, on the day of the party, probably in the afternoon, he'd got hold of those films. And the films were damned important. They were dynamite. Although I hadn't examined them I knew that. Sammy had known they were on to him and he couldn't trust a goddam soul. He couldn't get in touch with me because Janine was hanging on to him like a leech. He daren't get in touch with me in case he gave me away. They were on to him, but he was going to keep me out of it as far as he could. He came back to Kinnoul Street before he went to the party, and being Sammy he did the job right in the enemy country. My guess was that he got into Auntie's room and stuck those films behind her picture before he went to the party. He was relying on me to get enough sense out of his letter to realise that the operative place so far as I was concerned was the Kinnoul Street dump. Well, I'd got on to it and even if it was by luck that didn't matter one goddam.

I began to feel tired. One way and another I'd had quite a day. I looked at my wrist-watch. It was nearly three o'clock.

I experienced a peculiar feeling of elation. I had the definite idea in my head that when the Old Man had got those films enlarged we should be right on top of it. I grabbed the flask from my hip pocket and was delighted to find it was half full. I took a long pull and felt even better.

I went over to the doorway and switched off the light.

I was stepping out on to the landing when I heard a noise.

Somebody was opening the front door downstairs. I heard the click of the key and footsteps in the hall. I stepped back into the bedroom, closed the door, moved over to Auntie's bed and lay down on it. I lay there in the darkness waiting.

The steps came up the stairs. They were neat, light and definite footsteps. A woman, I guessed. I heard the tap of high heels on the landing outside and the sound of the door opening. Then the light went on.

Janine came into the room. She did not look in my direction. Her eyes were on the bay window, the black-out and the desk.

And she was a picture.

She was wearing a powder blue velvet frock under an open mink coat. There were shell pink georgette ruffles at her neck and wrists. Her small, high-heel feet were shod in bronze leather shoes, and those very attractive ankles in gossamer silk stoockings. Definitely a picture. An oil painting.

She turned and saw me and her right hand came up. In it was one of those small but very efficient Lugers with a " noiseless " bulb barrel that the Late Mr. Heydrick invented and issued to the German " I " people before a rather nice Czech knocked the gentleman off.

I grinned at her. I said : " Hallo, Janine. So glad to see you. I suppose you've come round to settle up about that little matter of rent ! "

CHAPTER NINE

BETTINA

I PUT my hands behind my head and relaxed. Janine stood at the bottom of the bed, her arms resting on the oak bedrail. She looked amused and slightly angry.

I said : " Well, Gretchen. How are things with you ? "

She smiled—a small sardonic smile. Her finger, I noticed, was well round the trigger of the Luger, and the idea occurred to me that she'd just as soon shoot me as talk to me.

She asked in her low, musical voice, with the slightest inflection of contempt : " Why Gretchen ? "

I said : " Because that's your name or something like it—Gretchen or Karla or Leisl—or some other not so nice German name. Unless, of course, you've got one of those new Nazi names that they're issuing out to children these days."

She shrugged her shoulders. She looked very beautiful, very tough, and very sinister. She said : " What are you doing here ? "

" Exactly the same as you are," I replied brightly. " I'm looking for the same thing. One of these days I'm going to find it. Even if I have to take the floorboards up."

" I don't think so," she said. " In fact I don't think you're going to look for anything—anywhere—after tonight. I think you're going to be dead."

" That's too bad," I said. " But I've heard that one before. They tell me that threatened men live longest."

I sat up on the bed and propped myself up against the pillows. As I moved she brought the muzzle of the pistol up. When I relaxed against the pillows she dropped it again.

" Listen, Janine," I said. " Why don't you be clever and give this up. You're beat and you know it. You've been stooging around with your friends Mrs. Bettina Vaile and Auntie and The Great Ravallo, and any other members of your travelling circus, for long enough. Why don't you give it up and try and save your skin while you've got the chance. I'm wise to you and even if you squeezed that trigger it wouldn't really get you anywhere."

She raised her eyebrows. She said : " No ? Tell me—exactly what do you mean when you say that you are wise to me."

I said : " Just relax and listen to me. If you're a sensible girl you'll take my advice and do what I tell you. My name is Michael Kells. I'm an agent working for this country. I've been doing it for years. More importantly, I was the one who was with Sammy Carew—-who you know well—too damned well—was on the French coast with the German Rocket Batteries.

" Well . . . we decided we'd done our job and we planned to get back. Carew went first. I was to follow him. In the meantime your friend Mrs. Vaile—I don't know what her German name is—had got wise to, and killed, an agent we'd sent up to Peenemunde. I think we just got off in time.

" My idea is that you picked Sammy up on the way back ; in France, I should say. That's why you pulled that stuff about being married to him abroad on me—remember ? You picked him up and you pulled a very old-fashioned one on him. You told him that you were working for the British or the French Resistance or something like that. You knew he wouldn't take that at its face value. So you embroidered it with a little bit of truth—just to sell the rest of the story. You told him a perfectly true story about a German Himmler External Section that was working over here trying to get information on direction and range of Flying Bombs and Rockets. You knew he'd fall for that one. You knew he'd fall for it if you gave him proof that what you said was true. Well ? "

She smiled slowly. She said : " Go on. You don't know how funny you are, Mr. Kells. So I gave him some proof of what I said ? "

" You could afford to." I grinned at her. " You knew once you'd got him over here, believing in you, you could get that proof—whatever it was—back before anyone else but Sammy had seen it. You knew that you could finish him off before he had time to do a thing about it. The only thing was—and this was rather tough for you—Sammy took you for a ride. Sammy was no fool. Anyhow, he was clever enough for you."

She said acidly : " Really . . . and what did he do ? "

I shrugged my shoulders. " For some reason best known to himself, Sammy was doubtful about you. In spite of your story, in spite of what you'd given him. You thought that he'd carry it on his body and that when you knocked him off you could get it back. But he didn't. He did a rather clever thing. The night on which he took you to

the Marinette party he did the thing—whatever it was—
in this house. And that was the cleverest thing he ever did
in his life. Sammy had an idea just before he went to that
party that you and your friends were out for him. You
knew he'd never had a chance to get rid of the documents
or papers whatever they were. So he planted them in
this house. After the party he took you home and your
friends were on his tail all the time. Every moment of
the day and night they'd been watching him. And he
knew it. Then after he'd dropped you at Verity Street
he came back here and drank a whisky and soda that
Auntie or somebody had carefully hocked. He went out.
When he came to there were people going over his room.
But they didn't find anything. Because Sammy wasn't
such a fool as to hide something in his own room."

She smiled. She said : " You're a wonderful guesser,
Mr. Kells, aren't you ? Or a wonderful liar. I suppose
you're going to tell me in a minute that you know where
he hid the documents ? "

I shrugged my shoulders. " If I'd been Sammy Carew
I should have hidden them here—in this room." I said.
" Because this is about the last place where anyone would
expect them to be hidden. As I told you I shall probably
start by taking up the floorboards."

The pitying smile came back. " Oh no, you won't,
Mr. Kells," she said. " I don't think you'll ever take
any more floorboards up. Incidentally, I wonder what
your *real* name is."

" I told you that before," I said. " Santa Claus."

" Very appropriate," she said. " But this time you've
got yourself stuck in a chimney. One that you won't get
out of."

" I'll get out of it all right," I said. " I'm not worrying
about me. I'm worrying about you. By the way, did you
have a good time at Miss Carew's place ? Did you find
out what you wanted ? Did you discover who Sammy's
boss was ? I'm rather sorry for you, Janine. You're not
doing so well—are you ? "

She sighed. She said : " If I were to tell you that I
was working with Sammy Carew ; that he trusted me
implicitly, I'd probably be wasting my breath——"

I said : " You don't have to worry about that. First of all, I've always distrusted you. I believe you worked yourself into Sammy's confidence, and anyhow I'm not taking any chances on you. There's just a chance that you might be telling the truth, but I don't think you are. At one time I had an idea that you were. Now I don't believe it. The weight of evidence is against you."

" Doesn't exactly the same process obtain in your case ? " she said. " Of course it does. Sammy never mentioned you to me. Never mentioned your name ; never mentioned——"

" You bet he didn't ! " I said. " Sammy wasn't such a mug. If he'd trusted you he'd have told you all about me. But he didn't. The reason is obvious."

She put slim fingers over her mouth and yawned. I began to move my hand in the direction of my breast pocket. Once I could get my fingers on the Mauser it would be worth my while taking a chance on trying to take a pot shot at the gun in her hand. But I didn't get the chance. The barrel of the Luger in her white hand came up and I moved my hand away quickly. I didn't fancy the idea of getting shot up at the moment.

There was a silence. Then she said : " Well . . . Mr. Santa Claus Kells . . . where do we go from here ? "

" So far as I'm concerned I don't intend to go any-where," I answered glibly. " This is going to be my per-manent address. I'm going to stay around here until something happens. And if I stay here long enough it's *got* to happen."

She said : " It will happen much sooner than you think." She moved away from the bottom of the bed, into the centre of the room. She stood, the pistol hanging down at her side, looking at me.

" You *might* be all right," she said quietly. " But it's odds against it. I believe you're playing a very clever game, Mr. Kells, and I'm not taking any chances on you."

I said : " That suits me perfectly. I'm not taking any chances on you either. By the way, how did you get to know where Sammy's aunt—Miss Carew—lived ? "

" How do you think ? " she asked. " The only possible way I could have known was from him."

"Nuts, Janine," I said. "You forget the picture post-card under your blotter, round at Verity Street. That picture postcard was one of a series printed years ago. It was probably sent you as a tip-off by one of your German friends who knew that Sammy used to stay with his aunt when he was in England. Sammy wouldn't have given you a picture postcard. He'd have given you the address. But why don't you go? You're beginning to bore me a little."

"You're talking rubbish," she said. There was an undertone of anger in her voice. "Absolute rubbish. I tell you that Sammy Carew gave me that address."

"And you also told me that he was married to you, and a few other sweet nothings," I said. "Listen, Janine. If Sammy had trusted you he'd have handed over those documents to *you*. He wouldn't have hidden them where *nobody* could find then. He'd have handed them over to you and told you what to do with them—where to take them. Even if he knew he was going to win it from your friends he'd have got rid of those papers. But he couldn't. He wouldn't give them to you, and he couldn't tell me where they were. He couldn't tell me at the party because *you were with him—watching him like a cat*. See?"

She said: "But *you* think you're going to find them. The clever Mr. Kells. *You* think you know where they are."

I grinned at her mischievously. "I've got a pretty good idea," I said.

She moved suddenly. She came a little closer. She said: "I've got a pretty idea too. . . . I've been trying to work out just where he *might* have put them. I think I might be right. And you wouldn't move . . . would you? I'm a very good shot and I should hate to kill you. You're such an *amusing* man."

"Go ahead," I said.

She backed towards the mantelpiece. Then she stopped, came over to the bed, put her hand inside my jacket, took out the Mauser from my breast pocket.

"You'll be much safer like that," she said. "You're much too impulsive to carry a gun."

She backed towards the mantelpiece. She put the

Mauser on the end of the writing desk ; stood, still facing me, sliding her hand along the mantelpiece towards Auntie's photograph. She picked it up, threw it into the fender. The glass broke ; the back fell out. The small brown envelope lay just inside the fender.

She stooped down and picked it up. She was smiling. Then she straightened up and came a step or two towards me.

" It looks as if my guess was right, doesn't it, Mr. Kells ? " she said. " It looks as if my guess was better than your guess."

" Look, Janine," I said casually. " Let's be friends. Let's do a deal about this thing."

" Like hell," she said. " I've got what I wanted and now I'll leave you to your thoughts." She put the envelope in the inside pocket of her coat.

" I'm going now, Mr. Kells," she said with a smile. " And you're going to stay just where you are, and I'm going to lock you in, and by the time you've got out of this room I shall be a long way away."

I didn't say anything. I thought that suited me perfectly well. I said : " Well . . . it's been nice seeing you. You might let me have that rent sometime."

She smiled. " I'll make a point of it," she said. " Unless I forget. You're not having much of a time, are you, Mr. Kells ? Which is a pity in one way. Especially for a man with your powers of imagination."

" My powers of imagination aren't so bad, Janine," I said. " Sometimes I think they're good. One of these days you might get the same idea."

" I *might*," she said. " But I don't think so. Well . . . good-night. . . ."

She moved towards the door. She opened it, stood, looking at me over her shoulder. I put my hands behind my neck and lay there, grinning at her. I was very glad she hadn't bothered to look inside the brown envelope. When she did she was going to be very surprised.

As it was, she was rather pleased with herself. She threw me a delightful little smile. She said :

" Really, Mr. Kells, or whatever your name is, you're an awfully stupid man."

I said : " Am I ? Do tell me why ? "

She said casually : " All your arguments and theories have been based on the fact that Sammy Carew hid this envelope in this room. The fact that *someone else* might have hidden it has never occurred to you."

" All right," I said. " Who else ? "

" Who but *me*, stupid ? " she said. " *I* hid it here. That's why I knew where to look for it. And good-night to you ! "

She passed through the doorway, closed the door. I heard the key turn in the lock outside.

I lay back and looked at the ceiling. I thought that by and large something might happen in a minute. Something good—for a change.

I waited for ten minutes ; then I got up, picked up the Mauser from the writing desk, broke open the door, went downstairs. Outside, the street was deserted. I walked along to the car, started up the engine, smoked a cigarette whilst it warmed up.

Then I drove to my apartment ; put the car away and went to bed.

I was asleep when the Old Man came through at noon next day. When I heard the telephone jangling I knew *something* had happened. I hoped it was going to be good.

It was. He said : " You're getting on, Kells. Congratulations."

I said : " Thank you very much. How well am I getting on ? "

" You'll see," he answered. " They're working on those films now. We shall have the enlargements done by sometime this afternoon or early evening. I'll send you a set round by Special Branch Despatch Rider. Then you can really get going. Good-bye."

I hung up and went back to bed. It seemed to me that just at the moment that might be the safest place for me.

At three o'clock the telephone rang again. It was Guelvada.

He said : " Hey . . . Mr. Kells . . . this ain't quite so good . . . but what could I do ? You know it's tough trying to keep on somebody's tail when you haven't got any assistance. I——"

I interrupted. I said : " You mean you've lost Auntie. She's given you the slip. Don't worry. I thought she would. What happened ? "

He said : " You were right. She went back to the cinema stage door during the early part of this afternoon's show. She went in and she came out damn quick. I had to be in the passageway—somewhere near—in case she went off in the other direction. I was in a doorway and she passed me so close that she could have touched me. When she was a few steps away she turned and gave me a goddam nasty look. I think she was on to me. Then she went along the main alley into the High Street. She crossed the road, went into a store and, I suppose, went out the back door. Anyhow, I lost her. So what ! Not so good . . . hey ? "

" It doesn't matter, Ernie," I said. " Not now. You'd better come back immediately. Call round here at my apartment at about eight o'clock to-night."

He said : " O.K., Mr. Kells . . . I'll be there."

The next time the telephone rang it was five o'clock. Freeby came on the line.

" I'm glad you're back," he said. " I came through to you yesterday. I'm worried about this job."

" What's worrying you, Freeby ? " I asked. " Isn't our very charming Mrs. Bettina Vaile doing what you want her to do ? "

" She's not doing anything at all," said Freeby. " That's what's worrying me. This woman ought to be scared. She ought to be trying to make a getaway, or line up with her friends. Isn't that right ? Well . . . she's just doing nothing at all. She's living at her flat, going out and doing a little shopping when she feels like it. She's be-having like any normal woman—and she doesn't seem to give a dam' about anything."

" That's all right," I said. " You've got to realise that she's a very clever person. My bet is she knows that you are on her tail, and she's just sticking around keeping you busy. She believes that whilst we concentrate on her we won't worry about anything else. Just keep on as you are and telephone me if anything really interesting happens."

I took a bath and a cold shower, drank a little whisky, dressed myself in some fresh clothes and smoked cigarettes.

At seven o'clock the Special Branch Despatch Rider arrived with a large envelope. I signed his receipt, gave him a drink and got rid of him; took the packet over to the window; opened it.

The top enlargement was a letter. I took one look at the handwriting and began to feel just a trifle excited. The handwriting was that of Collison—an agent who had worked with me on two or three jobs at the beginning of the war. Collison had been dropped in France a year ago and went underground. Nothing had been heard of him and we all expected that he'd been knocked off.

The letter stated briefly that the attached documents had been secured from enemy sources by a person who had been working with Collison and acting as *liaison* between him and the French Resistance. This person (said Collison) was entirely reliable. The first of the documents he continued, was a list of an enemy " External " Section that was already planted in England, with at least one known address per person and the names under which they would be living in England.

I took a quick look at the list and was amused to find that Mrs. Bettina Vaile was none other than Fraulein Liesl Ernst. There was a description of the lady so there was no doubt about it. I checked quickly through the list and identified Auntie with the blue eyes, The Great Ravallo, the white-faced boyo that I'd shot. There were two or three others that I knew nothing about.

The second document was a copy of an original German " I " order issued to this group with instructions as to what they were to do, the information they were to obtain about the ranges, directional flights, and hit sequences of Flying Bombs and Rockets. Nothing was said about how they were to get the information back when they'd got it, but I could probably guess the answer to that one.

The third document was a copy of another German " I " order relating to finance of the group and there was the usual stuff about people being expected to kill themselves if they fell into the hands of the English in order that no information should be extracted from them.

The fourth document was a map of Surrey done in rather a peculiar manner, and showing certain concentration points.

I went back to the Collison letter. He went on to say that he had been able, through the co-operation of a French Resistance unit, to get all the documents and his letter photographed and reduced on to small films ; that he would keep one copy, and that his associate who, he hoped, might be able to get to England within a reasonable period, would have the other copy. He pointed out that this person would be in a position to give certain other additional information on arrival which would probably be of value to us.

I put down the letter and lit a cigarette. Definitely we had got a break. With this information and the bits and pieces I'd managed to collect we could pull the job off. I felt very good and mixed another whisky on the strength of the situation. Then, with the glass in my hand, I wandered back to the table and finished reading Collison's letter.

There was only one short paragraph to read. And I read it and got the shock of my life. I stood there, with the whisky in my hand, looking at the words and wondering what sort of a mug I'd been.

For the last paragraph of Collison's letter said that the person who had originally obtained the documents, who had negotiated the photography with the French, was a lady who had, since the war, been working with the H.Q. French Underground Intelligence group. He attached a photograph of her and a description.

And the name was Miss Janine Grant !

The Old Man mixed a fresh whisky and soda ; brought it over to me and went back to his armchair. He drew on his cigar and blew the smoke out of his mouth slowly—watching it. He shrugged his shoulders. He said :

" Of course it's damned hard luck on the girl. But

what else could you have done. It's just one of those things."

I said : " I know. Just one of those things. At the same time I wish it could have been played differently. You ought to see this girl. She's got something."

He shrugged his shoulders again. He said : " Maybe I shall. I hope she still looks pretty. It's my guess you'll find her body in a ditch, or a river somewhere. They won't be very nice to her, you know."

I said : " I know."

" Carew wasn't in a position where he could *really* trust her," the Old Man went on. " He didn't believe in her and he didn't disbelieve in her. It's a pity that there wasn't more time for people to sort each other out."

" They never had a chance," I said. " Work it out for yourself. This Janine picks up Sammy on his way out of France. She doesn't know him. She only knows what he *says*. And that's all he knows about her. What she says. They both think they'll wait until they get over here where they'll be able to get to know the truth. In the meantime she had those films and she stuck to them. She didn't hand them over to Sammy because she wasn't sure of him. That's where I made my first slip-up. I always thought Sammy had those films."

" That was natural," said the Old Man. He swallowed some more cigar smoke.

" Then things moved too quickly for both of them," I continued. " Sammy discovered that the white-faced boyo was on his tail. He realised that somebody was on to him. He began to suspect everyone—including Janine. He was dead right. But he wasn't going to let her out of his sight and he took her along to the party. When he got there he didn't like it a bit. So he got tight as a tip-off for me ; and he didn't say anything about me to her. She didn't know a thing about me.

" Then things began to happen. Sammy was killed and I went round to see her. She began to be scared. She didn't know who Sammy was working for ; who his boss was. I was hanging about the place being tough and looking damned suspicious. She made up her mind she was going to hide those films and she did it cleverly. The afternoon that Auntie came round to see her she slipped out the back way, dashed around to Auntie's and hid the films behind that old so-and-so's picture. I thought, of course, that she'd gone round to go over Sammy's things."

"Well . . ." said the Old Man. "It's tough but there it is. There's nothing you can do about it."

I thought : "Can't I . . . Like Hell I can't . . ."

I finished my drink and I went. I knew exactly what the Old Man wanted done and I knew exactly what he'd say and do to me if I allowed myself to be deflected. Well . . . probably I *was* going to be deflected. Not much but just a little bit.

It had to be done. It had to be done because of a conclusion that I'd come to. And that conclusion was that I was rather interested in Janine—from a personal angle —if you get me.

I spent a little time walking about in St. James's Park thinking things over. It was now nearly half-past eight. Ernie Guelvada would be waiting for me at my apartment, impatient to be at something or somebody. I hoped he'd help himself to a drink. On second thoughts I knew he'd do that anyway.

I came out into Piccadilly and began to walk towards the park. I'd just made up my mind to get a taxi-cab and go home when a car pulled up at the kerb beside me and a rather nice voice said : "Michael . . . dear . . ."

It was Bettina Vaile—otherwise Fraulein Leisl Ernst— and she looked delightful. She was wearing a lime green rather close-fitting frock, with a short summer ermine coat.

I went over to the car. I said : "Well . . . I'll say this . . . You've got the nerve of the devil, Leisl. But where do you think this is going to get you ? "

She said smilingly : " I'll tell you, Michael. I'll tell you *just* where it's going to get me. And you are a very attractive and delightful man—even if I did have to shoot you with a gas pistol. Believe me, it was awfully necessary at the time."

I said : " Well . . . what is it ? Have you come along to give yourself up ? "

She pouted prettily. " No, Michael," she said. " I've picked you up here because I think we ought to have a drink together. Do you remember when you gave me dinner at the Berkeley. Such a delightful mug, weren't you, dear ? "

I said : " Any drink that I ever give you will have poison in it."

" Possibly, sweet," said the *fraulein*. " But I think its going to be very definitely to your advantage to give me that drink and listen to what I have to say. It's going to be a great help to you."

I looked at her. Her eyes seems a trifle less hard. And she was worried. I got the idea that Bettina or Leisl— whichever you like—was scared.

I said : " What are you going to do ? Sell out ? "

She nodded. " There isn't anything else to do, is there ? " she said. " We're on a bad wicket. I know it. The rest of us aren't inclined to believe that. They still think we can win and pull out of here. I don't. I don't believe in fairies. I never have."

" In other words, you're thinking of little Leisl," I said. " You want to make a deal ? "

She nodded again. " Yes, Michael," she said seriously. " I want to make a deal."

I opened the door and got into the car beside her. She was wearing a very attractive perfume. I looked at her sideways. I was right in my first impression, I thought. She was scared. She'd come to the conclusion that there wasn't any way out and she was going to do the best she could for herself.

I said : " How is it possible for you to make a deal ? You're a damned dangerous woman. You're a German, a spy ; you've probably done in half a dozen good Englishmen. . . ."

" Who would have done *me* in first if they'd had the chance," she interrupted. She swung the car round into Berkeley Street and pulled into the kerb. We got out and walked across the road into the Buttery. I ordered cocktails.

She said : " I don't believe that anything is ever quite hopeless. I still think that there is hope for me. I'm an Austrian and, whether you believe it or not, I was forced into this wretched business. Lots of women are spying and working as *agents* for the Germans. They *have* to. They don't want to. Well . . . I'm one of them and I don't see why I shouldn't try to save my skin."

I said : " As skins go it's rather a nice one to save. But tell me, what was it brought you to this point of view ? What's the sudden scare about ? "

She shrugged her shoulders ; made a moue. She said : " You, I suppose. I know you're too good for us. I know you've got something up your sleeve and I don't think that any of us have a dog's chance of getting out of England. I feel that. And I don't want to die. I want to continue living. Possibly when this war is over life may be worth living."

" You're making me cry, Leisl," I said. " But I'm still listening. What's the deal ? "

" The deal is this," she said in a low voice. " You must promise me that I shan't be shot ; I don't mind being put into prison for a little while. That I can bear, so long as I know that one day I shall be able to live my own life again. If you promise me that, I'll tell you everything that you should know now. I'll tell you exactly what our group propose to do. I will tell you what information they have and how they hope to get it back to Germany. And I will take you down—you and your friends—into the country and show you the place where they will meet —all of them—when the work is finished."

" When is the work going to be finished ? " I asked. I finished my drink ; signalled the waiter for some fresh ones.

" It is practically finished now," she said. " If you are going to succeed you must move quickly—very quickly. But first of all you must promise me——"

" Nothing," I said. " I'm not promising you a goddam thing, little Leisl. And even if I did, my promise wouldn't be worth the breath. You don't think I'm such a damned fool as to make a deal with you . . . do you ? "

She shrugged her shoulders. The expression in her eyes was piteous.

I offered her my cigarette case ; lit her cigarette and my own.

I said : " Listen to me. My advice to you is to talk now and talk all you know. That's my advice. Without my promising anything or making deals or anything else like that. If you've any information that might be of any use to me I *might* try and do something about you. I *might*. I don't say I shall. You'll have to chance that. Well . . . are you going to talk ? "

There was silence for a minute. Then she said : " I'm in your hands. I must do what you say ? "

I asked : " How many of you are there in this group ? "

She said : " Now . . . not many. There was, first of all, the woman who controlled it . . ."

" A woman of about forty or so with very blue eyes ? " I asked.

She nodded. So that was Auntie. I'd always thought Auntie was a big shot.

She went on : " And there was a woman whom you met at my party—a Mrs. Helsdon—a good-looking woman. And there was me. There were three women only. Now the men : First of all there was Karl—who was the young man whom you shot and put in the packing case—and there was a man called The Great Ravallo. He was an imitator of voices and he was engaged in going round the smaller cinemas. He had been in this country for years. It was always easy for him to arrange to appear at some place in which we needed information."

I looked at her. " Where is The Great Ravallo now ? " I asked.

" I don't know," she said. " He has disappeared. We do not know where he is. But that is not important. There was only one other place which he was supposed to visit. Such information as he had collected would already have been put into our leader's hands."

" Is that everyone ? " I asked.

She shook her head. " There are three more men," she said. " And to-morrow night the whole group will meet at a house in the country. A house that has belonged to one of us for years. There the final arrangements will be made."

I drank my cocktail. " And what do you propose ? "
I asked. " Will you take us there ? "

She said : " Yes . . . to-morrow night. The house is
near Andover. It is called Forest End. And it must be
approached by a certain route in a certain manner.
Otherwise there will be suspicion. You understand ? "

" I understand," I said. " Now listen, Leisl . . . I'm
going to take a chance on you. I think you're a pretty
bad specimen, but I'm still going to take the chance. To-
night—at a time we shall arrange—I will meet you and
you can take me down to this place. But no funny business."

She said : " I swear that everything I say and do from
now on is true, Michael. Thank you for giving me a
chance to prove that I mean that. Now listen to me, and
I will tell you what we must do. . . ."

I ordered some more cocktails and listened.

I stood outside the Berkeley and watched Leisl's car
disappear in the direction of Berkeley Square. I lit a
cigarette and began to walk back to my apartment.

Well . . . now I knew they'd got Janine. They were
going to make her talk. And just so that they should be
uninterrupted in the process they were prepared to sacrifice Leisl. The story she told me was of course rubbish.
It was her job to get me and anybody else to Andover to
give them the time and the freedom they wanted to
finish the job.

But she was good. She was a good actress. She was
tough. She had nerve.

When I got home Guelvada was sitting in the armchair,
drinking whisky and soda. He was well dressed and
looked very much the man about town.

He got up, put his heels together and made his usual
punctilious little bow. He said : " You know, Mr. Kells,
I'm goddam sorry about this Auntie woman. It isn't
often I make a slip-up . . . hey ? But what could I do ?
You can't tail a woman successfully unless you have two
or three people working with you."

I said : " Don't worry your head about that, Ernie.

169

I've told you that doesn't matter. Incidentally, if you're feeling particularly murderous I think you're going to get a chance."

He said : " You mean at last I'm going to get a chance to kill somebody. I—who in this business have been nothing but a stooge up to the moment."

I said : " Well . . . I think somebody's going to get their throat cut. I hope it's not mine."

I gave him another drink. Then I said : " I've just had a very interesting conversation with one of our German friends—Mrs. Bettina Vaile, who is Leisl Ernst. She has decided to sell out her friends. She's decided that to-night she's going to take us down to Andover where the rest of the group is meeting. All I have to do is to promise her that she won't be shot."

Guelvada grinned. He said : " The old stuff, hey ? They're still using this woman as a red herring ? "

I said : " Maybe. But it's not going to get 'em anywhere. Finish your drink. Get on to Freeby and tell him to come round here. We've got to get organised."

CHAPTER TEN

THE BOSS

ERNIE GUELVADA, slumped back in the driving seat, with two fingers on the wheel, sang an old and rather rude Flemish song. It occurred to me that he was happy. Happy, I supposed, to come to the conclusion that the time was arriving when, with a bit of luck, he might have a chance of killing somebody. I hoped so too.

I began to wonder about my guesses ; just how far they were going to prove right—or wrong. Just what would happen if they were wrong.

If they were, it wasn't going to be so good for Janine. Not so good.

I began to think about Sammy and his last twenty-four hours of life. They must have been pretty exciting. More especially as he couldn't do anything very much except let events take their course—which is something that nobody—at least nobody who is any good—likes doing.

I'd got a pretty good idea in my head about those last twenty-four hours. Neither Sammy nor Janine could have had a very good time. Neither of them knew who they could trust—or not trust.

Guelvada put his foot down on the accelerator and the Old Man's Jaguar shot forward and settled down to a good sixty. We had passed Thilford, and when I looked at my watch I saw it was just after eleven. Anyway, even if I was right, we were cutting things a bit fine.

I looked at Guelvada sideways. He was still singing his bawdy song ; smiling a little. By his left foot, almost under the driving seat, was the small attaché case that he had brought with him ; that he handled a little carefully. I had an idea about that attahce case and understood his idea in bringing it. He'd probably been thinking about the old days and that girl of his . . . the one in Belgium.

I put my hands in the pockets of my light overcoat, and relaxed in the deep seat. Janine, I concluded, had picked Sammy up somewhere in France. Probably on the coast, where the fishing folk were inclined to be helpful. She'd discovered that he'd fixed to get back to England and she'd told him her story but, because she didn't know too much about Sammy, had said nothing about the films. I thought that, at that time, her attitude was probably right.

And Sammy had arrived knowing about the Himmler External Section that was operating in England ; believed it enough to make up his mind to do something about it ; but not enough to trust Janine entirely. So they were both in a spot.

Then, very soon after they'd arrived in London, Sammy realised that he was being tailed by the white-faced boyo. That fact, not extraordinary in itself, made him a little more careful and told him that somebody was on to him. He made up his mind to get cracking on the job ; telephoned to the Old Man and said he was on to something, asked were I was going to be when I got back. His one idea was to get me in on the job because two heads are better than one, and he wasn't quite certain what Janine was really after.

She, on her part, was watching Sammy like a cat. She was taking no chances. She'd had the films, probably somewhere on her body, and she wasn't parting with those until she knew just where she was.

Then White-Face, insolent, and taking a chance to get away with it and get Sammy identified by his friends, had the nerve to suggest to Sammy—probably over a drink at The Heap of Feathers—that Sammy should go to the Marinette party. Sammy had jumped at the chance. At least it might give him something tangible to start on. Probably he'd asked if he could bring a girl friend. So he took Janine. Also he rang through and, finding that I'd arrived, asked for me to go along too.

Then when he'd got there, before my arrival, he'd seen the thing that had scared him. I had a pretty good idea of what that was. In his letter he'd talked about the woman who was beautiful ; who had scared him a bit. This was someone he'd seen before and therefore it couldn't have been Janine. It was a blonde. My guess was that the blonde was Mrs. Helsdon and that Sammy had seen her sometime in France, working for the Germans or up to no good anyway.

So he'd got tight. This was a tip to me, and when I'd arrived I'd followed suit.

Probably this didn't please Janine too much. She couldn't understand what it was all about, and it didn't make her any more keen on Sammy.

After the party he'd taken her home to Verity Street. Somebody had been on their tail and Sammy knew it. So did Janine. Either Sammy had told her or she guessed it. Probably the latter. She was scared now. She wanted to get rid of those films and she didn't know what the hell to do with them. She was in a spot.

Then Sammy said good-night and went off home ; drank his doctored drink like a little gentleman and passed out. Woke up to find people in his room—looking for something. He must have wondered what ! He'd made his final gesture ; been carted off somewhere, kicked around a little and killed.

That was Sammy that was !

Now Janine was in a real spot. Next day things began to happen. She was told that Sammy had been killed by the Flying Bomb. Maybe she believed it and maybe she didn't. It didn't matter what she believed or didn't believe. Sammy—her one contact in this country—was dead. She didn't know a goddam thing about him ; she wasn't even certain if he was straight. She probably had as many arguments with herself about Sammy as I'd had about her.

After which things began to develop in a big way. I appeared and began to ask questions about Sammy. She became more and more distrustful of everyone ; she believed that it was her business to find out about Sammy before she did anything else. Quite obviously, she knew where Sammy lived. Maybe she'd tailed *him* sometime. She was scared of me and she was waiting for something else to happen.

Some girl Janine. She had something else besides that face and figure and personality. She had nerve. I hoped she was going to continue having it !

The next thing to happen to her was Auntie. Janine, no fool, realising that they'd taken the trouble to tail Sammy to her place, knew that sometime or other they would be snooping around to find out just where she came into the story. She just stayed around and waited. Then Auntie appeared. It was obvious to me that in the meantime Janine had kept her eyes on Sammy's place. She'd done that because he'd never appeared after the night of the party. Maybe she did not distrust him so much now ; thought that somebody might have got at him. Somehow during that time she'd see Auntie—either coming in or going out of the place in Kinnoul Street.

And definitely Janine put Auntie on the other side. She didn't like Auntie a bit and she was dead right !

Then Auntie appeared in Verity Street. She decided to go and see Janine. Auntie was worried because White-Face disappeared and they hadn't got around to finding him.

Janine had a bit of luck for a nice change. She'd seen Auntie in Verity Street, obviously looking for the house, and she decided to take a chance. She got out by the back way, slipped round to Kinnoul Street behind Auntie's back, probably with the idea of seeing if she could get in the place and find out what had happened to Sammy. When she did get there she discovered Sammy's clothes nicely piled on the bed ; his trunk on the floor. One look told her that somebody had taken the linings out of his coat and sewed them in again not so neatly. That gave her a few ideas too. She went upstairs, discovered Auntie's picture on the mantelpiece ; came to the conclusion that this was *her* bedroom, stuck the films behind the picture because she was damn certain that nobody would ever look *there* for them and got out.

And if I'd had the sense to realise that *she* had the films —*and not Sammy*—I might have saved myself some headaches, and she wouldn't be in the spot where she was now.

I began to think about The Great Ravallo. I'd been a trifle stupid about The Great Ravallo. Obviously, he'd been used to imitate Sammy's voice to Miss Carew, Sammy's own aunt, and quite obviously he was the boyo who had telephoned through to Bettina Vaile's flat, spoken to Alison Fredericks, imitated *my* voice and got the kid to go round to Namur Street where they'd discovered White-Face's body in the packing case, not so much by luck but because everybody in our game knows that an empty house or a " To Let " is the easiest place to knock somebody off or hide a body. They knew White-Face had been knocked off in the Mulbery Street district and the rest was easy.

But the important thing was that The Great Ravallo was able to imitate *my* voice. *That meant that he'd heard it.* And that meant that he'd been at the Marinette party, which was the only place where he *could* have heard it.

And that was that !

I was playing The Great Ravallo as my final bet and I hoped it was going to come off.

The Jaguar was doing a steady fifty-five. Guelvada started a new song. He stopped crooning suddenly. He said:

" So you're certain that the key to the whole thing is Ravallo . . . hey? You think that so-and-so is the one ? "

I said: " Work it out for yourself. Ravallo was the agent detailed to go around the country. Every place mentioned in that date book of his was a place well inside the Flying Bomb area. Except one place . . . the place we're going to."

He slowed down for a hairpin bend. " And this place is the place for the pay-off ? " he asked.

I nodded. " People working in the External Section in specific places could report to Ravallo when he came round. His business was to collate those reports. He had that done when he was playing the Cinema at Walling. Walling was the last place for him to pick up a report. During the time he was there he did the job ; finished his survey of the whole business and handed it over to——"

" My God . . ." said Guelvada. " I believe you're right. He handed it over to Auntie. That's why she was there."

" I hope I am right," I said. " If I am, I take it that this place is the last meeting place. Here the whole job will be tied up and the information will be sent, by some means or other, from here."

" And the girl . . . Janine ? "

" This is the most obvious place for her to be sent to," I said. " Work it out for yourself. When she went down to see Sammy's aunt at Chippinsfield she wanted to know where to take those films ; and the right person to receive them. She told Miss Carew the story and Miss Carew told her that an instruction had been received for her to go down to Pellsberry, go to The Weathervane Club and hand over the films to the individual who will be indicated. Of course these people haven't any idea as to what is in the envelope. But they know she's got something. They've made up their minds they're going to have it and that she's going to talk to them and like it ! "

Guelvada said: " That could be. But what happens when they find just a few pieces of paper in the envelope. It's not going to be so good for her . . . hey ? Not on your goddam life ! "

" There's a chance," I said. " A good chance. Anyhow, we'll soon know. Besides, this *ought* to be the night. It's the time when I'm supposed to be on my way to Andover with our good friend Mrs. Bettina Vaile. I had to be got out of the way so that they could have a clear field down here."

Guelvada grinned. He said : " I would like to see her face when she arrives at the meeting place and instead of meeting you she finds herself pinched . . . some surprise! I bet she'll use some language, that one . . . hey ? "

" I bet she will," I said. " I could imagine the expression on Bettina's face when she discovered that, instead of succeeding in taking me for a ride, she'd merely taken herself for one. I wished it were possible for me to be there and watch. I wondered just what she'd do. If I knew anything about her she'd probably put a bullet through her head. And a damned good riddance !

We slowed down as we ran into Mayton. Outside the little town, where the roads forked, Guelvada stopped the car at the edge of the grass verge.

Freeby came out from the shadow of an oak tree. He came over to the car. He said :

" It looks as if you've guessed right this time, Mr. Kells. The Weathervane Club is on the main road to Forbridge outside Pellsberry—about a mile outside. It used to be an old farmhouse. It's owned by a Mrs. Mayne who's been living in the house beyond it—there's only one house near it—for the last six years. She arrived here about a year before the war started."

I asked : " Anything else ? "

" Yes," said Freeby. " They've got an extension on to-night. Dancing goes on until two o'clock. They're giving the proceeds to a local charity."

" How far is Mrs. Mayne's house from The Weathervane Club ? " I asked.

Freeby considered for a moment. Then : " There's the Clubhouse, standing in a bit of ground. Then at the back there's an open space used for parking cars—when people have got cars. This space is about twenty or thirty yards long. On the other side of this space is a little thicket, and Mrs. Mayne's house stands in that. You could throw a stone from the Club to her house."

"All right, Freeby," I said. "You get back to town and take a night off."

He said : "I hope I'm not going to miss anything."

"Nothing that you wouldn't want to miss," I said.

Guelvada started up the car. Freeby waved his hand. We went on. The road curved in and out of the low hills. Ten minutes driving brought us to Pellsberry.

"Drive round the town," I told Guelvada. "Hit the main road on the other side. I don't think we want anybody to see us from now on. Not until *we* want to be seen."

Guelvada nodded. He said : "Believe it or not I am beginning to be just a little excited—just a little." He grinned at me.

We circled the town ; came out on the main road on the other side. We ran over a hill and into a valley. The road twisted and turned through the valley with the green hills on each side. A moon had come out and the hills were a mixture of shadow and silver.

As we rounded a curve, I could see, half a mile away, the two houses.

"Pull into the first side turning and park in a field or in some bushes," I said. "We'll finish this on foot."

Guelvada swung the car over a little bridge on a road that led away to the left ; turned into a dirt track through a gate. He stopped the Jaguar in the shadow of a hedge. We got out.

There was a bulge under Guelvada's coat and he carried the small attaché case in his right hand. He looked as happy as I have ever seen him look.

We walked down the road keeping in the shadows. A few minutes brought us to the end of the field next to The Weathervane Club.

The Club, an old-fashioned farmhouse, stood in a clearing just away from the road. From where we stood the wind brought the sound of a hot melody to our ears. I was glad that they were still dancing.

"This is where we separate," I told Guelvada. "You get round to the back of the Club, check on any cars that are there. Try and find some sort of concealed passage or subway leading from the Club to the house. It's pretty certain that there's going to be one."

Guelvada said : " And where do I find you ? "

I grinned at him. " How do I know ? " I asked. " When you've done what I told you, you'd better come and have a look. I'll be around somewhere. Maybe inside the Club."

He said O.K. He went off.

I skirted the field, keeping in the shadow of the hedges, worked my way round the edge of the clearing and approached the Club from the back. The sound of the band came from the far side of the house and I imagined that the dance room and bars were on that side and that there would be kitchens and store-rooms on this side. I moved quietly along the back wall, trying to identify doors, listening for sounds from within. There was complete silence on this side of the house.

I found a window that was set up a good five feet from the wall. A pantry window, I thought. I broke the lock off and wriggled through. I replaced the blackout ; flashed my torch. I had been right. I was in a large pantry. Bottles and provisions of all sorts were stored around the shelves. The door was unlocked.

I pushed it open. Now I was in a larger store-room, and I could hear the sound of the music—the band was playing a *rhumba*—distinctly.

I opened the door on the other side of the room. The music became louder. Before me stretched a long passage with one or two doors on either side. At the far end was a heavy curtain.

I moved quietly along the passage. It was obvious by the sound of the music that the dance floor was on the other side of the curtain. As I passed each door in the passage I stopped and listened. I heard nothing. If anybody was inside they were keeping very quiet.

I reached the end of the corridor, and drew one side of the heavy curtain an inch from the wall. In front of me was a large room which had been converted into a dance room. The band—a five-piece band—was in the far corner on the right and there were tables set all round the floor. The tables and chairs were gilt and the general set-up of the place made it look like an inferior imitation of what, in pre-war days, was called a night club.

The curtain behind which I was standing covered what was evidently a service entrance to one corner of the room. There was some sort of gallery above, and the corner was in the shadow. I moved the curtain a fraction more and took a look round the room.

I had guessed right!

At a table set apart from the others on the right hand side of the floor, well away from the band platform, a supper party was in progress. Auntie—her face wreathed in smiles—sat at the top of the table. On her right was Janine. On Auntie's left was the beautiful Mrs. Helsdon ; next to her was the girl Miss Varney whom I had also met at Bettina Vaile's party. There were three men—young and tough looking specimens—whom I did not know.

As I watched, Auntie turned her head and looked towards the main entrance to the dance floor, which was diagonally opposite to my corner. She looked at the door and then at her wrist-watch.

I smiled to myself. So far so good. They were waiting for someone. Someone important. Probably the boss. I replaced the curtain carefully and retraced my steps along the passage, through the store room, into the pantry and out of the pantry window. I edged round to the cleared space where one or two cars were parked and made my way towards the hedge on the other side, behind which Mrs. Mayne's house stood.

Guelvada came out of the shadows behind the hedge. He came close to me. He said : "There is a covered way from the Club to the garage here behind the house. Of course there will be a door in the garage which leads into the house. Come with me. I'll show you."

He led the way along the hedge. Fifteen yards inside the hedge and built on to the house, was a brick garage. A covered passage led from it, along the edge of the parking space.

"This leads to the side entrance of the Club," said Guelvada. "So that if it's raining anybody can walk from there to the house without getting wet. Also it prevents any one leaving the Club and coming here being seen from the main road. A good idea . . . hey ? "

I nodded. We moved into the shadow of the garage wall. At one end, propped behind a bush, was Guelvada's small sub-machine gun. Beside it was the attaché case.

" What's in the attaché case, Ernie ? " I asked him.

He spread his hands. " You know," he said slowly, " I am always prepared for the worst. . . . No one ever knows *exactly* what is going to happen and sometimes a little explosive—not too much but just enough—is very useful . . . hey . . . when the party is large ? "

I said : " We were right. Janine's here. They're waiting for someone. My guess is that when that person arrives they'll come along to the house—all of them. I'm going back to the Club just in case they decide to play it some other way. Stay here and see if you can unlock and lock the garage door. I've an idea we shall want to get in there."

Guelvada said, grinning : " I've already done that. It was so easy it was a joke. O.K. I'll stick around here and wait for you."

He went back into the shadows.

I made my way back across the clearing, through the pantry window and along the passage. Luckily such service as was going on—and it was mainly drinks—was being conducted from the bar which stood in the corner by the main entrance. Nobody seemed to be using this passage.

I pulled the curtain aside and took a look. The supper party was still in progress and Auntie was leaning over, with a charming smile on her face, talking to Janine. I began to think about Sammy and made a wish about Auntie. Not a particularly nice wish.

Two or three minutes went by. Then a man came over from the entrance. He was wearing a doorman's uniform. He spoke to a woman sitting at a table near the supper party. When he had finished she got up, spoke to Auntie, followed the man back to the main entrance. Auntie got up and stood by her chair smiling towards the doorway.

A man came in. He looked the perfect specimen of the English gentleman. His clothes were right, his moustache was right, everything about him was distinguished and quiet. Behind him was the woman who I guessed to be Mrs. Mayne—the proprietress of the Club.

Auntie went to meet him ; brought him to the table ; began to introduce him to the party. He sat down and a waiter brought him a drink.

The band began to play another hot number. People got up and started to dance. I was glad about the band. It was pretty certain that my supper party friends weren't going to try and do business in that atmosphere, which suited me very well. I needed quiet as much as they did.

I put the curtain back, leaned against the wall, waited. After a minute a man came down the passage from the direction of the store room. He stopped dead when he saw me. He said: " Who——"

I hit him. Once. I put everything I had into the punch. He fell against the opposite wall and was beginning to slither down when I caught him. I slung him over my shoulder and carried him back to the storeroom. I propped him up in the pantry, closed the door and went back to the passageway. I thought it would be a good ten minutes before he was interested in anything at all—if then.

I took another look through the curtain. The supper party was still going strong. One of the men was dancing with Mrs. Helsdon ; the rest of them were talking. The distinguished-looking late arrival had now parked himself on Janine's left ; was engaged in earnest conversation with her.

The music stopped. There was a pause and then every one got to their feet and the band played " God Save the King."

I grinned to myself. I stood there, my eye stuck to the crack between the wall and the curtain, watching a bunch of Nazi agents standing for our National Anthem. The idea pleased me a lot.

Now the music had stopped and the band had already begun to pack up their instruments. Auntie, who had sat down after " The King," got up and looked round at her flock. They got to their feet and began to move—not in the direction of the main entrance as the other people were doing—but down the left-hand side of the Club. Guelvada had been right. They were going to use the covered passage.

I moved quickly down the passage, through the storeroom into the pantry. I flashed my torch on the face of the man lying against the wall. He seemed quite disinterested in life. I left him there, scrambled through the window, raced round the edge of the car clearing, along the hedge. Guelvada was waiting behind the garage.

" They're on their way," I said. " Take it easy, Ernie, and don't start anything until I give you the tip."

He said O.K. very softly.

A minute passed. We stood there in the shadow watching the end of the covered passageway where it finished on the edge of the coppice. Then I could hear the sound of voices becoming louder as the party approached.

Janine and the last arrival came out of the passage and moved across to the garage door. I could hear him talking to her.

" . . . of paramount importance to this country, indeed the whole Empire, Miss Grant," he was saying.

Auntie, who came next, moved in front of him. I heard her opening the garage door, fumbling with the key.

The rest of the party followed them.

We waited. I heard the sound of the garage door being shut and the voices inside died away.

" We wait two minutes," I said.

They seemed like two hours. I nudged Guelvada and we moved round to the garage doors. He worked quickly and efficiently on the lock. It took him another minute. We pushed the doors open, went in, closed them behind us, leaving them unlocked.

On the far side of the garage were two steps and a green painted door. I tried it. It was unlocked. I opened it an inch or two and stood, in the half darkness, listening. From somewhere in the house I could hear the murmur of voices.

Out of the corner of my eye I could see Guelvada leaning against the wall of the garage, his tommy-gun and attaché-case on the floor beside him. He was manicuring his nails with a small Swedish knife, an instrument with which, I had heard, he was very effective. He was smiling.

Then, quite suddenly, he stiffened. I looked over my shoulder. The man I had left in the pantry had pushed open the garage door and stood, on the threshold, holding his jaw, looking at us. The moonlight showed us the expression of astonishment on his face as he saw us.

Guelvada made a little hissing noise between his teeth and threw the knife. It struck the man full in the throat. He fell sideways, tearing at the hilt of the knife. Then he lay still.

I said : " Nice work, Ernie. Close the doors. Guard the fort here for a bit ; then work along the passage until you find me.

He nodded. I pushed open the door, stepped into the passage ; began to move, very slowly, very quietly, in the direction of the murmur of voices. As I moved towards a crack of light at the end of the passage I could hear Auntie's voice and the sound of a quiet laugh.

I came to the door. I opened it an inch or so, and looked round the edge. The room was a sitting-room. On the other side was a heavy curtain forming an entrance to another room. I moved across the room and stood with my ear to the curtain, listening.

The man was speaking. The man who had been the last arrival at the supper party. He said :

" Enough of this fooling. My friends, we will get down to business. I welcome you all here to-night. *Heil Hitler !* "

There was a soft chorus of *Heils* and a gasp. I grinned. That would be Janine.

Someone said : " Just stand quite still where you are, Miss Grant. That is if you desire to continue living."

I looked over my shoulder. The door opened and Guelvada came over to me. He walked like a cat, noiselessly. He was grinning.

The voice went on. It said : " You know, Miss Grant, you are a most unfortunate young woman. First of all I am certain you have always tried to do what you consider to be your duty to your country, but then so do we.

From the first, when your association with the late Mr. Carew, was noticed, we suspected you. When you went down to see his aunt, Miss Carew, at Chippingfield, then we knew that we were right.

"Incidentally, we had guessed you would go down there. We've known for a long time that when he was in this country Carew used to stay there. Obviously his aunt knew what he was doing. So we arranged a little plot for her and for you. A colleague, who has a flair for imitating voices, telephoned Miss Carew, said that he was her nephew, that you were not to be told where the instructions came from, but that you were to bring any documents you had down here.

"So, first of all, Miss Grant, let us divide this interview into two parts. You have certain documents. We want them. . . ."

Janine said : "I will never give them to you—never."

I heard Auntie's cold and incisive voice : "She's probably got them on her."

The man said : "Very well. Search her. I'm sorry we have to do it so publicly, Miss Grant. . . ."

Janine said in a choked voice : "It seems I have no choice. I'll give them to you. . . ."

There was a pause. I imagined the unfortunate Janine handing over her brown envelope. Then the man said :

"Very clever, Miss Grant. But where are the real documents ? Inside this envelope as you see are three pieces of paper."

I heard another gasp. Janine was having a night of surprises.

I slipped the Mauser out of my pocket, took off the safety catch. Behind me, Guelvada stood, the tommy-gun resting on the crook of his arm.

The voice said : "Miss Grant, I will give you two minutes to tell me where the original documents are. Incidentally, it may interest you to know that in this case which you see on this table are the collated reports from our agents in this country, collected at such risk by a colleague of ours, who rightly called himself The Great Ravallo. To-night this case will go to a place known to us on the coast ; thence to France and Germany. You will understand, Miss Grant, that I now desire to add to it those documents or pictures which you have. Where are they?"

I didn't wait to hear any reply. I pushed aside the curtain and stepped into the room. They were standing round a table, Janine facing her questioner. Auntie looked at me, and her face turned to chalk.

I said : " Sorry to interrupt this little party."

The man who had been questioning Janine turned towards me with an oath. I don't think I've ever squeezed a trigger with such joy in my life. The bullet hit him in the chest ; knocked him sideways.

I grabbed Janine's hand, yanked her through the doorway. My second shot smashed the electric light bulb.

I said : " Guelvada, take 'em." And, as I dragged her through the room into the passage, I heard the chatter of his tommy-gun.

We raced down the passage, through the garage, through the hedge and across the clearing. On the other side, near my pantry window, we stopped. Janine leaned against the wall gasping.

I was worried about Guelvada, but I need not have been. He shot through the hedge ; then went over on his face. He was wise. At that moment his time-bomb went, and with it went the residence of Mrs. Mayne and the remnants of Mr. Himmler's External Section.

I breathed a sigh of relief.

Ernie Guelvada, who was driving, slumped back in the driving seat and crooned one of his rather peculiar Flemish ditties.

I turned towards Janine in the back seat, wrapped the rug a little more closely about her. The night had become colder.

I said : " Tell me something, Janine. Why did you put those films behind the picture at Auntie's place in Kinnoul Street ? Weren't you taking a bit of a chance ? "

She said : " What could I do? When I saw her coming down the street, I made up my mind to get out the back way, to go round to the Kinnoul Street place to see if I could find anything—anything that Sammy Carew had left. While I was there I heard someone at the door. I had the films on me. I thought that if it were one of those people I might lose them. My one idea was to put them somewhere. That seemed to me the best place. I intended to come back for them."

I said : " Well, you did. Do you remember that interview we had in Auntie's bedroom ? "

She said: " I shall never forget it, Mr. Kells." She was smiling.

I said : " Don't you think you might call me Michael for a change ? Mr. Kells is a little formal."

She said : " I agree—especially having regard to the fact that you have always called me Janine. But perhaps you've forgotten our original interviews ? "

I said : " I shan't ever forget them. I hope there'll be a lot more—possibly just as original."

She sighed. She said : " I'm afraid there will be."

I looked at Guelvada. He was looking ahead at the moonlit road, grinning.

I said to Janine : " Why ' afraid ' ? "

She looked at me sideways. She said : " Perhaps you remember that I also told you at our first interview that I considered you to be the type that very often gets what it wants. . . ."

Guelvada began another song.

In the distance we could hear the noise of fire-bells.

Guelvada stopped singing. He said : " There must be a fire some place. Maybe somebody dropped a doodle-bug." He laughed. " Is that goddam' funny or is it . . . ? "

He continued singing.

I said to Janine ; " I take that last remark of yours in the spirit that it was meant. . . ."

She interrupted. She was smiling. She said " Don't misunderstand me, Michael. I said I considered you to be the type that *very often* gets what it wants. I didn't say *always*."

I shrugged my shoulders. I gave her a cigarette and snapped on my lighter.

I said : " Janine . . . what's a *word* between friends."

THE END

>>> If you've enjoyed this book and would like to discover more great vintage crime and thriller titles, as well as the most exciting crime and thriller authors writing today, visit: >>>

The Murder Room
Where Criminal Minds Meet

themurderroom.com

9 781471 901799